She lay in bed, eyes wide open, and truly awake.
These sounds were real. They *had* to be.
They were coming from outside her window.
The dog was barking. There was a train in the distance.
This wasn't a dream.

She rolled out of bed, crouched by the window, and peeked out from the bottom corner of the window, careful to keep her head outside the frame. Across the way, she saw the two small windows of the barn squinting back at her like dark, empty eyes. The buggy stood next to the barn door, in its usual spot. But the barn door was half-open, which was not usual. In front of the barn, the yard was empty. But it was a shimmering, charged emptiness, a vibrating darkness.

Something ran by. Rose heard the rapid footsteps. She saw a blur. Now the dog was barking even louder. She raised her head a bit. She needed both eyes. She was barely breathing or blinking. She didn't want to miss it, whatever it was. Something was out there. Someone. There were nights, and even times during the day, when she was certain he was near. Sometimes, in the fields, she was certain that she was being watched. She could feel it in her body. In her joints. In the little hairs on the back of her neck.

Also by Dana Becker

Searching for Rose

Published by Kensington Publishing Corp.

FINDING ROSE

DANA BECKER

ZEBRA BOOKS
KENSINGTON PUBLISHING CORP.
www.kensingtonbooks.com

ZEBRA BOOKS are published by

Kensington Publishing Corp.
119 West 40th Street
New York, NY 10018

All Kensington titles, imprints, and distributed lines are available at special quantity discounts for bulk purchases for sales promotion, premiums, fund-raising, educational, or institutional use.

Special book excerpts or customized printings can also be created to fit specific needs. For details, write or phone the office of the Kensington Sales Manager: Attn.: Sales Department. Kensington Publishing Corp., 119 West 40th Street, New York, NY 10018. Phone: 1-800-221-2647.

First Printing: June 2022
ISBN-13: 978-1-4201-5190-9
ISBN-13: 978-1-4201-5191-6 (eBook)

10 9 8 7 6 5 4 3 2 1

Printed in the United States of America

Chapter One

Rose lay in bed, perfectly still. Sometimes at night, at the end of a long, exhausting day on the farm, her body would sink into a grateful sleep, but her eyes remained wide open. There would be images and voices so vivid, they could only be real. Images whose undeniable realness, however, evaporated the moment she found herself waking up. Only to realize it was all a dream.

But this time it wasn't. She lay in bed, eyes wide open, and truly awake. These sounds were real. They *had* to be. They were coming from outside her window. The dog was barking. There was a train in the distance. This wasn't a dream.

She rolled out of bed, crouched by the window, and peeked out from the bottom corner of the window, careful to keep her head outside the frame. Across the way, she saw the two small windows of the barn squinting back at her like dark, empty eyes. The buggy stood next to the barn door, in its usual spot. But the barn door was half-open, which was not usual. In front of the barn, the yard was empty. But it was a shimmering, charged emptiness, a vibrating darkness.

Something ran by. Rose heard the rapid footsteps. She saw a blur. Now the dog was barking even louder. She raised her head a bit. She needed both eyes. She was barely breathing or blinking. She didn't want to miss it, whatever it was. Something was out there. Someone. There were nights, and even times during the day, when she was certain he was near. Sometimes, in the fields, she was certain that she was being watched. She could feel it in her body. In her joints. In the little hairs on the back of her neck.

She'd moved out to this farm in the middle of Amish country, west of Lancaster, with April and Joseph, her sister and her brother-in-law, to heal. She would learn the farm life. She would live on country time. She would help April open her new restaurant. She would build a new world away from her old life in Philly. And slowly it was working. But there were moments of backsliding, of relapse. Of utter fear. The healing was slow, but the backsliding . . . that happened rapidly, and without warning, like an ambush. One moment the slow comforts of health buoyed her, and the next, she was suddenly thrown into the middle of a foaming, frigid sea, thrashing about, choking on salt water, drowning. At other times, the experience was something else altogether, something beyond even fear.

She saw the boot first. For one brief second it flashed next to the barn door, and then was gone. But she saw it. Her heart raced. Someone was in there.

The feelings suddenly took over. The feelings she never told anyone about. The feelings she barely admitted to herself.

It's him, she thought.

And the feeling that came with that thought wasn't fear or dread or horror. Rather, it was the feeling that lurked on the other side of fear; it was where fear leaves you when it is done with you. It was agitation and excitement. It was the painful pleasure of anticipation. And with it, a spiral of irrational thoughts. *He's come for me. He promised he would, and now he's making good on it. They say he's evil. But I know the truth. He's special. He sees me for who I am. He'll bring me back to the compound. Back to the Community. Back* home.

For a moment Rose savored these secret thoughts, savored this moment, allowed her heart to clench with anticipation at the thought that she would be restored to the good graces of Whitey. She stood up and set herself squarely in the middle of the window, to see better. Who cared if he saw her? Rose *wanted* to be seen. She stared out the window. She bored her eyes into that barn door, trying to will it open, to reveal herself to him.

I'm here, she whispered in the dark.

She considered turning around, running downstairs, and flying out the front door. Running to him and taking nothing with her. Begging for his forgiveness, begging to be brought back home.

"*Rose.*"

She jumped and bumped her head against the window frame.

"Didn't mean to startle you, hon," April said, standing behind her, leaning against the doorpost.

"It's okay," Rose said over her shoulder, but still looking outside.

Outside, the fullness of the dark had drained away. It no longer shimmered. Now it just seemed empty and quiet in the yard. And Rose's secret thoughts evaporated, too. For a brief, lucid second, she felt guilty about her excitement to see Whitey again. But just as quickly the guilt was also gone—forgotten, as though it, and the thoughts that caused it, had never existed to begin with. It was as if she had just woken up and immediately forgotten the dream she was having. Seeing her sister's tired, worried face brought her back. She smiled.

"Don't worry, Ri," Rose said. "Just having some trouble sleeping."

She saw the skeptical, sad look on her sister's face.

"I'm *fine*. Really. I'm okay. I'll be asleep in a minute. You don't need to tuck me in."

"Joseph said he saw you looking out the window," April said.

"Oh, that was him out there. Well, I'm allowed to look out the window, right?"

"He said you looked . . ." April didn't finish the sentence and seemed to regret bringing it up.

"What?" said Rose. "That I looked what?"

April sighed.

"It doesn't matter."

"I'm tired," Rose said. "And anyway, I was looking out the window because your dude was creeping around in the middle of the night."

April sighed again.

"You're right. He shouldn't do that."

"What *was* he doing out there?"

"We—or I . . . tonight was my night—I forgot to secure the coop. Joe saw a coyote out there and ran over to get things right before there was trouble. Got there just in time."

After they said their good nights, Rose climbed back into bed. And just as she drifted off to sleep, she heard voices. It was April and Joseph. She could hear their voices coming through the grate in the floor. They must have been in the kitchen, right below her room. Her body was heavy, and already succumbing to sleep. But her head guided itself to the edge of the bed. She flopped over, facedown, so that her ear was poised right at the edge.

"So," she heard April say, "what was it?"

And then Joseph's lower voice, muffled, said something.

"You sure?" April said. "It was *him?*"

Joseph coughed. He either didn't answer, or he was pausing. Or Rose simply couldn't hear him. She could feel herself drifting headlong into sleep.

"No," she heard Joseph's voice say finally. She was struggling to stay awake, to hear what he was saying. "But it *was* someone," she thought she heard him say. And then sleep carried her away.

Chapter Two

Rose barely needed a trigger to bring her back to That Day. And as soon as her mind was there, the whole scene returned to her as though it were still happening. Whitey had personally woken up Rose that day.

When he'd first kidnapped her, he'd treated her the way he treated all his captives. But he had taken a special liking to Rose. It seemed he was strangely drawn to her. He'd gotten into the habit of waking her up himself, quietly unlocking her door so he could crouch next to her bed, watching her as she pretended to sleep.

He wasted no opportunity to tell her, once again, that she resembled his sister Hefsibah. His beloved sister Hefsibah. The wronged Hefsibah. The greatest heartbreak of his life, Hefsibah.

He'd told her the stories so many times she could recite all the details. Hefsibah had been the second youngest of twelve siblings, originally from Wayne County. One afternoon, when Hefsibah was twelve or thirteen, she collapsed during her chores. No warning. She just fell to the ground. She'd been hauling a pail to the barn, to replenish the goats' water supply. And the next second, she was lying flat on her face, with the overturned bucket beside her, spilling out its contents all over her dress.

Nothing would revive her. Not smelling salts, not cold water. As luck would have it, the family happened to know that a community doctor was nearby that day, making a house call at a neighbor's. So one of the young men in the house jumped on a horse and went to fetch the doctor immediately.

But the doctor, too, could not revive poor Hefsibah. It wasn't long before he determined that it was too late. There was no pulse. She was gone.

In those days, as Whitey explained to Rose, the Amish of this area rarely used the local hospitals. Usually they went to the hospital only for serious chronic illness or for surgeries. For most other cases, they used home remedies and their own doctors. In Hefsibah's case, they might have rushed her to the hospital, but there was no need: the girl was dead.

Hefsibah was buried in the family plot, behind the barn of the original family farm, which was down Stony Creek Road, only a short ride from where Hefsibah had lived with her family. Her extended family was almost too shocked to mourn. And anyway, Christian modesty and decorum were tenets of their community—every member of the family, following the lead of the parents, was committed to accepting this terrible loss as the will of God. Everyone but Gabriel, the little boy who would grow up to become the notorious Whitey. Years later, when Whitey would tell Rose this story, he would always arrive at the same conclusion: his belief that Rose was somehow his sister.

He was the youngest of the family, the only sibling

who was younger than Hefsibah. Only a shade over a year older, Hefsibah had been his best friend and closest ally in the world. Little Gabriel was inconsolable upon her death. He denounced, as a traitor, anyone who tried to console him. Worse, he cursed God. He would not accept the simple fact that his sister was gone forever. Someone was lying to him. And he wasn't having it.

After Hefsibah was buried, Gabriel remained by her grave all afternoon, refusing to leave. And when, one by one, his family left the graveside, his rage deepened. He couldn't believe that his family was just going to leave his sister outside, in the ground, as if she were an animal. Gabriel vowed, then and there, that he would never forgive his family for this betrayal of his sister. They told him that she was dead. Her soul was in heaven. Her mortal life was ended. But, in his mind, his sister was alive.

Gabriel kept his furious vigil into the night. It was a humid summer evening and he wasn't about to go inside. He curled up on her grave, on the freshly turned soil, and dozed off.

That's when it happened. At first, he thought he was still asleep. But he wasn't. He was awake. He could see the sky and the dark shapes of the barn and pens and fields. He could smell the farm aromas. He was at his grandfolks' house. He was awake. No question about it. And the sounds he heard were real.

It was a low sound. The thrum of a heartbeat? Was it possible? No, ridiculous. Not a heartbeat, not a regular rhythm. But something. A distinct pounding of some sort. From the grave. Gabriel pressed his ear against the fresh, still-moist soil, and put his hand over his other ear, canceling out all other sounds. And when he did, the sound he heard from his sister's grave was even louder and more distinct. A knock; then nothing, then more nothing. Another knock. Two more knocks.

Gabriel lunged into action. He knew what he needed to do. He was a young boy then, only eleven or twelve. But he had a fierce personality and was also physically large. And the burial of his beloved sister—the unforgivable betrayal, in his mind, by his entire family—had filled his body with such a zealous rage that he became a fully grown man in one single night. When he heard the sounds—or what he thought were sounds—from his sister's grave, he ran to the barn, grabbed a pick and shovel, and began furiously digging. Though he didn't care for, nor trust, his family to help him, he knew that more people digging were better than one, and so he began shouting, even as he was digging.

It wasn't long before his uncles and cousins, and one of his brothers, came running out. Without even hesitating, they tackled him, certain in their suspicion that Gabe, already so troubled by the loss of his sister, had now finally gone mad. But Gabe was strong and filled with the righteousness of his cause. He put up a formidable fight. But soon enough his family members overpowered and subdued him. They had to tie him up and gag him. He would not relent otherwise.

But when they had Gabriel gagged and tied up, and the noise and commotion of the fight had died down, they heard it, too. They heard the same sounds that Gabriel had heard, the same sounds that had sent him, deranged, into the barn to grab a shovel. The sounds were unmistakable. When Whitey told Rose this story, he would re-experience the emotions of that moment—the torment and struggle, the horror.

The men and boys all stood there silently by Hefsibah's grave. They listened. And then it came again: the muffled sound of pounding. Without even saying a word to each other, they all ran to the tool shed, grabbed every pick and shovel they could, and furiously began digging. They were so focused on the sudden, horrifying task that they hardly noticed young Gabriel, still lying on the ground, gagged and hog-tied. But soon, one of them did notice and untied him. He immediately joined them.

Within minutes, they'd managed to dig far enough to hear more of what was happening down there. It wasn't just pounding. It was scratching. And most chilling of all: a small voice. It was a girl's voice, no doubt. But it sounded animal-like. No words could be discerned. And yet its meaning could not be more clear.

When they reached the casket—the very casket they'd buried only a few hours earlier that day—they hoisted it out of the ditch and threw open the top. What they saw in there was so horrible that none of them ever really managed to describe it directly. It was as if they'd forgotten what they'd seen. But they hadn't forgotten. They remembered all too well.

All of the people involved agreed, though, that what they witnessed changed each person there that night, each in his own way. None of them was ever the same. And they also agreed on another detail: Hefsibah's eyes. Yes. They were wide open. Wide, wide open. And her lips murmured continuously. Every few moments her mouth would drop open, and her eyes would screw up, as though she were shrieking. But not a sound was heard.

The moment they'd come face-to-face—again—with Hefsibah, one of the older boys, Gabriel's cousin, Reuven, panicked. Convinced that this was the work of the devil, he lunged at the girl, determined to suffocate whatever demon had possessed her body. The other men restrained Reuven. But he continued to rave that they had made a great mistake in unburying Hefsibah, they had to kill the demon, or immediately rebury this body—or burn it. The men, though some of them murmured that perhaps he was right, restrained Reuven and overruled him.

One of the men picked up the girl. Her body was almost totally limp, despite the intense alertness of her eyes. He carried her into the house. When Hefsibah's grandmother saw this, saw one of the boys walk into the kitchen with the girl they had buried that morning, she collapsed on the floor and fell ill for a week. She nearly died.

Hefsibah lived out the rest of her life on Stony Creek Road, just a short distance from where she'd been buried. She eventually married, had a few children of her own, and lived a life of average length. But she was always a strange, quiet presence. She said almost nothing. She rarely smiled. She had a look of doom permanently on her face.

Whitey had, at first, taken Rose captive simply as a matter of business. It was just another transaction in the life of a crime boss. She was the collateral for a debt incurred by her drug-dealer boyfriend. But then Whitey discovered who she was, that her sister was dating Joseph Young, a nephew from his estranged family. Then it became personal. He decided he wouldn't return this girl. At least not without demanding a price.

But Rose only heard about that after she'd been rescued. During her captivity, Whitey confided in her the real reason she had come into his life. He believed that some-how, some way, God had brought back his older sister, whom he loved more than anyone, and restored blooming life to her. Over and over, Whitey told Rose of the resem-blance to Hefsibah—the physical similarities were strik-ing. The red hair, the big green eyes, the slightly pouty lips, the small childlike nose. She *was* Hefsibah, he swore. And not only that. She was the Hefsibah he remembered so well, the one who was full of life, the Hefsibah before the incident, before the burial. In confused moments, when Rose's time in captivity had generated a fog around her mind, she wasn't sure herself what was true. Maybe Whitey was right. Maybe God had brought Hefsibah back; maybe Rose *was* her.

On that last morning, as on all mornings, Whitey slunk into Rose's room at four-thirty, before anyone else was up. He lit a small candle in a lantern, gently brushed her hair back from her forehead with his fingers, and whis-pered, *"Hefsi . . . it's time to wake up, darling."*

He took her hand and squeezed it tightly. He kissed her on the forehead. Just as he did every morning.

Except that morning was different. Somehow she sensed it right away, even before he told her anything. She couldn't have dreamed of what he had in store for her that day. But she knew that something was happening, something that would change her life forever.

"My brave, brave girl," he whispered that morning upon waking her. "What did I do to earn your love back?"

Whitey was in tears.

"Today is the day, my dear," he whispered as she opened her eyes. Whitey turned away and wept for a moment. Then, gathering himself, he repeated to her, "Today is the day, my dear Hefsibah."

She hadn't replied right away. But then she'd smiled. He could be so tender. And she was starved for tenderness.

He'd held a ritual for her in the main sanctuary. As everyone in the Community knew, the loss of his sister was the entire reason Whitey had started the Community. If it was indeed a cult, as people said it was, it was the Cult of Hefsibah. He had Rose lie down on her back in the center of the circle. One after another, each member of the Community took a turn walking up to her, kneeling beside her, kissing both of her cheeks, and whispering into her ear, "Good-bye, Hefsibah, we will see you soon."

Every single woman was in tears. Some sobbed openly. Whitey removed Rose for the last time. He bound her feet and hands with ribbons—*to keep you safe,* he whispered to her, and she nodded—blindfolded her, and carefully placed her in the back seat of his van. He drove her out to the site, near the creek, near his old family's house—which he'd purchased and kept empty, as a sacred ground. This was where his sister had been buried that first time. He sang the hymns that had so moved his sister as a child.

"Sing with me," he said. And she did.

After spending so much time with Whitey, Rose knew the words. And they were beautiful to her.

Even though she was submitting herself to die, she

didn't really think she would die. On the contrary, she truly believed she was about to cross over into a truer, more vivid kind of life. She had always believed in eternal life. This belief was, for her, a lifelong form of optimism. Whitey had hijacked that optimism for his own purposes. But he hadn't exactly brainwashed her. Rose's communion with that buried girl was something that had originated from within her. Her relationship with Hefsibah came about on its own, apart from Whitey's meddling.

Nevertheless, Whitey's account of Hefsibah, which he repeated to Rose, almost word for word, did make a strong impression on her. And often, new details would emerge in his retellings. He remembered seeing his sister's body laid out, dead—or so everyone had said. They were preparing her for burial. Her hair had been neatly combed and tied back in braids. She was wearing a Sunday dress. Her arms had been folded over her chest, her favorite bonnet folded in her hands, her eyes gently closed. She had looked so small, so slight. Gone was the energizing force that had given her life.

But she was still his sister. Hefsibah was *right there*. It was a phrase that he would repeat when telling this story, and it made a strong imprint on Rose's mind. Hefsibah was *right there*. Young Whitey had refused to accept his family's insistent claim that she was dead. Finally, when his father had lost patience with young Gabriel and said, *Enough foolishness,* his sadness and frustration had come together into something else: rage. It had suddenly and horrifyingly occurred to him that his father was deceiving him intentionally, and that the whole family had turned on him and on his sister.

This is the devil, Whitey told Rose when he got to that part of the story.

The devil was something he'd learned about from the boys around the farm. They hadn't learned about it in their own church. But there were neighbors, non-Amish Christians, who had talked about the devil. And the Amish boys were whispering about it, speculating wildly when nobody else was around, especially at night, when they went on secret adventures into the woods together. Yes, there was this thing called the devil, or Satan. It was a man, a force that could take any shape, and was pure evil. It could appear anywhere and do its work in unimaginable ways. One of the boys would say, "*It could be Teacher Ruthie. It could be your* daed *or your* mamm. *It could be one of us right here. It could be* you."

"*How do we* know who *the devil is, then?*" some boy would eventually ask.

And one of the other boys, the kind who always seems to have the answers, and always seems to have them immediately, would reply, *You* know. *When the devil shows you his face, you know it.*

Well, Whitey had looked at his father's face, which had been scowling down over him—even as his sister lay presumed dead, even as she was being prepared for burial. He'd looked closely at his father's face as he'd said, *Enough foolishness,* and what he saw there wasn't his father's face at all. It was a vacant look. It was the devil. *When the devil shows you his face, you know it.*

Gabriel had been sure of it. And his voice, too; it didn't quite sound like his father's voice, especially his tone. This was the devil showing himself. That was the moment Gabriel came to believe, with total certainty, that his sister wasn't really dead. That they were burying her alive. As it turned out, he was right about that part. And, to him, being right about that also proved that he was right about his father—that the devil had taken him. Gabriel believed that as a boy. And as a grown adult, who was more widely known as Whitey than Gabriel, he still believed it.

Of course, as a child no one believed him about anything. And there was no reason to believe him. The girl was quite clearly dead. Anyone who put their head on her chest could confirm it: there was no heartbeat. Had they kept their ear on her longer, they would have heard it, would have heard the impossibly slow beat, with long pauses between, the sign of her rare condition—but nobody did, and so they drew the natural conclusion. Her heart had stopped.

They ignored Whitey's growing fury. They forgave it and explained it as the pain of a sensitive young boy, unable to reconcile himself with the painful truth. But as he grew more upset, more defiant, more accusatory, and ultimately violent, they began to fear him. Feared what had come over him.

And that boy, Whitey, fully grown, had taken Rose down to the creek, to be baptized, and then buried alive. Or, as Whitey referred to it, "to be given over whole," to redeem her forever. And Rose had believed it. Not because she believed Whitey. But because she believed herself. She believed what the small voice inside of her had said. She believed Hefsibah, who'd become a real presence in her life.

After baptizing Rose in the creek, then drying her off with a towel, braiding her hair and putting her in a Sunday dress, he then gently placed her into an unadorned pine coffin, Whitey had been filled with the same rage he'd felt the day his sister was buried.

"How can they *do* this to you?" he had roared. "They will *pay*."

And in that moment he'd vowed to contact his nephew Joseph Young, son of his brother Hezekiah Jonathan Young, about his plan. *Let them come here,* he'd shouted. Let them suffer, the way that he had suffered. Maybe it would be good for them. Maybe in this way, they, too, would be redeemed. He'd said all of this and looked at Rose for approval of the plan. She did not object. (Was some part of her secretly hoping to be saved by Joseph and April? Rose, in thinking about it later, was never sure.) Whitey immediately dispatched one of his men to tell Joseph.

And just like that, in the next moment his rage completely disappeared, replaced by a painful tenderness toward Rose. Whitey sobbed heavily, from deep inside himself. Even later, when Rose had come to realize how much she hated this man, she could never quite bring herself to judge him for those tears. That pain was real. And she wasn't immune to the emotions behind it, the feeling of loss, of a bereavement with no end.

"Don't forget me, Hefsibah. Please. Please remember me," he had said between sobs as he closed the top of the coffin.

And after he'd shoveled all the dirt back over the coffin, Rose was certain she knew how Whitey was feeling. *He feels empty,* she thought. *And serene.* That was how she felt, too, in the darkest darkness she had ever known. When she couldn't tell whether her eyes were open or shut. Couldn't tell whether she was breathing.

Couldn't tell whether she was alive or inside the dream of death. She prayed to Hefsibah. It was the last clear thought she could remember having. Then something happened. She would never really know what it was. And the memory of it was so awful that it could never be excavated, much less verified. It was something that lived in the attic of her mind, scratching and shrieking and then going so silent that she questioned whether it was there at all. It was a bottomless paralyzing panic. Followed by a penetrating ringing in the ears that never really ended. And then a darkness deeper than the darkness of the coffin.

Rose would later find out what had happened next. And not because anyone wanted to tell Rose this story. But because Rose asked and asked again. She needed to know. After much coaxing, she learned what happened. When Joseph and April had first arrived at the scene, Whitey's footprints were still crisply impressed into the dirt. It was clear that he'd been there a very short time ago. Maybe just minutes earlier. This was a good sign, they'd believed. It was the closest thing they had to hope.

When he'd first seen those footprints, Joseph was suddenly overcome by a wave of sorrow—and horror. Not in his wildest dreams could he have envisioned, when he'd told April the ghost story that circulated within his Amish family, about the girl who was buried alive, that it would end this way, that they would be pulled into this nightmare themselves.

The ambulance had arrived. But when the medics jumped out, ready to go to work, Joseph informed them that his men were still digging. The medics stood by, watching in utter disbelief.

The men dug quickly and efficiently. They didn't exchange a word. There was no need. Everybody knew what needed to be done. And there was also a sense of awe, a kind of hushed understanding that what was happening here, the monstrous burial of a living person and the unburying of wet earth, and retrieval into the world of the living, was a kind of sacred, almost mystical act. Just as likely, of course, was the possibility of digging up someone who had no life left. When people spoke, they whispered. Despite the intense emotions and the heightened adrenaline rush, nobody shouted. For a few minutes the only sound heard was the rhythmic crack and swish of five shovels digging in tandem.

And then, a hollow thud. And then another. This was it. The men picked up their pace, quickly and feverishly shoveling out the last layer covering the pine coffin, cleaning away the soil from around the edges. Without a second's hesitation, the men threw aside their shovels and dove into the pit, grabbing the coffin by its sides and hoisting it up and out of the grave, laying it on the ground.

When questioned, April had confessed that she was almost too stunned to breathe at the sight of that coffin.

Her sister, Rose, was *here*. After so much time in captivity, Rose was right here, right now, just a foot away. Joseph grabbed April and held her tight, as one of the men fell onto the coffin and quickly jimmied it open.

Unable to move, or breathe, April just stared at the coffin. There was no movement inside and April couldn't bear to look any longer. Instead she looked at Joseph, trying to read his face as he looked toward the coffin. Based on his reactions, she would try to gauge what was happening inside that coffin.

At first he looked worried, then slightly panicked. It was clear from his face that whatever he was seeing was not encouraging. Without wasting another moment, Joseph and another man reached into the open coffin and pulled Rose out, the man holding her legs and Joseph hoisting her under her arms. They laid her gently on the ground. She wasn't moving. The medics ran in and immediately went to work.

Joseph was on his knees, behind the medics, watching Rose, as they listened for any breath, watching her chest to see if it was moving.

"We gotta do CPR," one of the men shouted.

"No, no," one of the medics shouted back. "She's breathing."

"You sure?" Joseph said.

The medic had hooked Rose onto a monitor and oxygen. He then turned to Joseph and nodded. Joseph watched a bit longer. And then smiled and gave a thumbs-up. And then, in a voice so weary it was almost a whisper, he said to April, "*Rose is alive. Her eyes are open.*"

Chapter Three

Rose woke with a start. The faintest light of dawn glowed softly on her window. The rooster was crowing. She groaned, rolled over, pulled a pillow over her head, and muttered, "Shuttt uppp" into the bedsheet. But in truth, she loved seeing that faint light of dawn, and she even loved that stupid rooster.

Rose was living two lives. By day, she was a person. She chatted with her sister. She did chores and took walks. By day, she was a person who lived in her body. By night, she wasn't that person, or any person: she was just a pair of eyes and ears. Just a jumble of senses and reactions.

When the rooster crowed, it wasn't just the start of a new day, it was a sign—clear material evidence—of her sanity. Hearing it instantly brought her a deep sense of calm. She could immediately feel her body relax and her jaw unclench. For the next hour or so she could get actual sleep, the kind that restored her—restored, at least, some part of her.

Her days were full. She liked to be involved with every aspect of the farm. First thing each morning, even before eating breakfast, she checked the crops, probably more thoroughly than was strictly necessary, walking up and down the long rows of corn, looking for withered stalks to remove, noting where the animal invaders had been. Then she'd clear brush and mend critter fences, check on the granary. These were things that Joseph had taught her to do. They were things he himself did daily, but she wanted to do them, too, to learn more. And for the routine of it.

Then she'd eat breakfast, made for her by April. Then she would tend to the animals, especially the goat, Esau, whom she loved even if the love wasn't always recipro- cated. She would feed and groom the animals, clearing their cages, harvesting eggs from the coops. In the after- noon, she would wander a bit into the forest with her dog, Darlene. She would forage for berries and mushrooms. If she got spooked, she'd return home. But this happened less and less with each passing week.

She rarely left the farm. Every other Friday April and Joseph would get into the buggy and drive the five miles to the town of Sugar Lake, to get some supplies and gro- ceries. Sometimes Rose would join them, but rarely did she go into the store. Instead, Rose would walk aimlessly up and down Sugar Lake's one street, looking into the shop windows. A woodwork and quilt shop was Amish owned. But it also seemed to be aimed at tourists who came through town. An Amish general store seemed to be aimed more at Amish customers. Most of the other shops seemed to be non-Amish, and not particularly in- terested in outsiders who came into town. Some shops, like the ice cream parlor, seemed to be owned by non- Amish people, but employed mostly Amish, and served both Amish and non-Amish. The town was tiny but seemed, to Rose, more complicated than Philadelphia. Each time she went into town and talked to people or, more commonly, eavesdropped, she learned a bit more. Often, though, she ignored the puzzle of this new setting and simply drifted off until she reached the bridge and the creek that ran under it. On warm days, she would go down there, take off her shoes, and put her feet in the shallow, ice-cold water, feeling it glide around her ankles, feeling the leaves and twigs bump gently against her in the stream.

On one Friday trip to town, however, she stayed close by, waiting outside the store for April and Joseph to return. She drifted off toward the spot where a few of the Amish buggies were parked, to get a closer look at some of the horses. Rose couldn't stay away from horses. She'd never spent much time around these creatures, but she was immediately and powerfully drawn to them. To their soulful eyes, to the way they were a bit frightening because of their size and strength. But yet, they were also so gentle and innocent. Rose had never seen an angel before, but she imagined it would be something like being in the presence of a horse, both comforting and a bit scary.

Rose stood in front of a horse that was a perfect mocha hue, feeling, as always, a bit jealous of the horse's long, lustrous eyelashes. She tried to muster up the courage to pet its mane.

"Hey there," a voice called from behind her.

Rose froze. She shrank into herself, her eyes shut, her fists clenched. She never used to be like this. But this was her reality now. She tried not to fight it, but to ride these waves of anxiety.

"*Hey*," the voice said again, a bit warmer this time. Rose relaxed just enough to open her eyes. She hadn't quite managed to unclench her fists.

"Didn't mean to startle you there."

Her heart was racing. But she forced herself to smile. Then she turned around.

The man was seated on a bench, next to a little girl, who was holding her bonnet scrunched up in her hand. The man was dressed in the Plain style: a dark plum button-down shirt, sleeves rolled up, navy blue broadfall pants held up by two suspenders, and brown work boots. He immediately tipped his straw hat back on his head, so that his entire face was visible. Rose was slightly surprised by this unexpectedly bold gesture, and she flinched, expecting to feel overwhelmed by his large presence, his gaze. But his eyes were so soft and sparkly, and his smile so boyish and inviting that her fake smile became a genuine one, and her fists relaxed. He looked familiar. She was certain she'd seen him somewhere but couldn't place him.

"That's old Jeremiah," he said. And when she didn't reply, he added, "The horse over there, I mean."

"Oh, yeah," she responded, finally getting some words out.

"He's a kind old geezer, a wise man," he said. "You can go ahead and pet him if you want. He's real friendly."

"Thanks," Rose said, not daring to pet the horse or even to move. She was certain that if she turned away now, she'd flee.

"Oh, look at that! I didn't even introduce myself," he said. "I'm Micah. And this here is little Becca, my niece."

"I'm not *little*," said Becca, "I'm *big*."

"Sorry! This is *big* Becca."

"Hi," Rose said, in almost a whisper.

A long awkward second passed. Rose wished she could sprout wings and fly. These interactions were so painful. She didn't ever know what to say. And they reminded her of her former self, a person who *always* knew what to say in this kind of situation. She used to be quick with a quip. Confident. Now she just seemed to be sinking into the ground with each passing moment.

Though she didn't dare make eye contact, Rose did peek up at Micah's twinkling eyes for a moment. He was still looking right at her. But there was no impatience in his look.

"What's your name?" Becca said, finally.

"Oh, yeah. It's Rose."

"That's so *pretty*," the little girl responded.

"How old are you, Becca?" Rose said.

"I'm five and a half and a little," she said very seriously. "For my next birthday we're gonna have a cake from Kroger. I already got it picked out."

Rose laughed. Micah did, too. And as they laughed, their eyes briefly met, before Rose turned away.

"We're drawing a *cat!*" Becca said, almost shouting.

She held up the worst picture of a cat that Rose had ever seen. It was clearly the work of an adult hand. It was what might be conventionally called ugly, even hideous. Every single line was wrong, and disproportionate. It was so monstrous, it was almost interesting.

"Wow," Rose said, pointedly trying not to look at Micah. "That's *some* cat."

Rose couldn't hold back a laugh. From the corner of her eye she noticed Micah flushing deep red.

"Yeah . . . well, that one was mine," he said.

"You don't say," Rose replied.

"I can build you a shed if you want, but my drawing skills . . . well, I don't have drawing skills."

Rose quickly turned her gaze toward Micah. For a moment their eyes met again, and they shared a smile. For a moment this meeting of smiling eyes felt entirely natural. For a moment, Rose felt completely at ease. And then, just as quickly, the moment passed. No, it shattered to pieces.

Rose turned away quickly. Her chest and throat constricted. She couldn't speak. She could barely breathe. She felt that she might burst out in tears. But no tears came. Instead, she just stared at the ground.

"Can *you* draw me a cat?" Becca was now saying.

Without turning her gaze, Rose could see Micah's strong hand reaching out toward her, holding a blue crayon.

"I, um . . . I . . ." Rose replied. She was literally holding her breath.

Rose could not say how long that moment lasted. Maybe it was a split second, maybe it was a painful minute. Rose would occasionally experience these moments, when she almost completely blacked out. Usually it happened when she was alone, in her room or in a field, and her thoughts overwhelmed her. But sometimes it

happened right in the middle of a social interaction. Rose
would just evaporate.

"Rose!"

She came to attention. She noticed that the blue crayon
had somehow ended up in her hand. April was calling her.

"*Rosie* . . . over here!" April called out. "We're ready
to take off."

April was standing in front of the store, holding two
shopping bags. She had a knowing look on her face, and
Rose immediately guessed what she was thinking.

"So . . . how's Mr. Micah doing?" April said, with a
raised eyebrow, once they were seated in the back of the
buggy.

Rose didn't answer. Or rather, she couldn't. Instead she
just stared out at the passing countryside, at the big bill-
board by the side of the road that advertised a phone-in
prayer service. There were times when language simply
wasn't available to Rose, and April knew that. She immediately dropped the question.

"I'm just being silly," April said, as she noticed the
curious blue crayon in her sister's hand. "Don't listen
to me."

But Rose was listening to her, even if she showed no
sign of it. She was also thinking about Micah. She barely
got a look at him. She did steal one glance, though, right
before she had turned around to join April. She had seen
his smile fade, as though he was disappointed to see her
go. *Yes,* thought Rose, *I think that was what it was*. In re-
calling it now, the faintest little smile crossed her own
lips. April, too, had seen it.

Chapter Four

When Joseph declared his intention to build a new set of stables, April immediately declared her opposition to the plan. Joseph reminded April that she grew up in South Philadelphia. What did she know about stables and barns?

"You can't tell me it's actually necessary," April said. "It's so much time and money. Are the horses *so* sad to stay in the barn? Do they really need their own separate building?"

"Yes, that is what they need," Joseph said. "They need more space. You don't want to live in the barn. Neither do they."

"And you know this?"

"Yup. Know my horses better than you, South Philly."

And when she gave him an unimpressed look, he added, with a vague note of pleading, This will be for *us*."

"Oh, right," April replied. "*Us*."

April may have still been a farmer-in-training, but she knew her man. She saw how he'd grown frustrated working for other people. She strongly suspected that Joseph had taken on this big project because he wanted to be his own boss for once. He wanted to be able to build something that he himself would use. She saw how difficult it was for him to build a beautiful shed or kitchen cabinets or barn for someone else and then walk away.

"Fine," she said. "But I'm gonna remind you that you told me 'This will be for us.' It'd *better* be."

Joseph wasted no time getting his crew together, a rotating group of six laborers, all but two of them blood relatives. One of those two was Micah. Micah was an all-purpose worker. He was big and could swing a hammer. But his specialty was detail work. He could make wood sing, and not only through carving but also by paying close attention to the nitty-gritty principles of carpentry. Joseph knew that when he asked Micah to do something, the result would be perfect. Often it would look even better than Joseph had imagined. When he decided to take on a big project, Joseph often brought on some of his brothers and cousins for extra hands. But Micah was there because of his talent alone.

And he knew it. And he let people know that he knew it. Micah had a slight tendency to boast. One of his former employers had nicknamed him Mikey Showboat. He couldn't help himself. When he finished making something, his very first impulse was to show it off. When he made Joseph and April a new kitchen table, he was so proud of it that that he called everyone in the house to gather in the kitchen for its unveiling. Rose had arrived just in time to see him jump up and land on top of the table in a full seated position. His hands were out-stretched, like an actor accepting a standing ovation at curtain call.

"How does it look?" he said. "Steady?"

But he knew very well that it was steady. The table did not move a centimeter when he jumped on it. It was as if he'd jumped onto a slab of stone. Rose, who was standing in the doorway, tried to suppress her smile at his theatrics. And yet, later that day, when she sat at the table, and ran her hand over its smooth edges, she was amazed. It was quite possibly the most perfect table she'd ever seen.

Micah had become one of her farm tutors. Because Micah was an incorrigible extrovert, he ended up chatting with her when she had questions about how to do something. More and more, Rose could be found lingering among the crew as they worked, to "learn more about how to build things." Construction wasn't generally considered a skill women on the farm were expected to do. But Rose was already enough of an outsider to Amish culture that the strangeness of her hanging around the workmen seemed no more odd than her presence on the farm to begin with. And, in any case, she was sincere in her desire to learn. She was also a quick study. It wasn't long before she was genuinely helpful to the crew.

Micah, in particular, found her to be very helpful. And before long, she was his right hand, helping him haul wood, helping him measure planks, handing him tools as he called out for them. They were a good team. Everyone noticed it. Rose and Micah, however, didn't notice that they were being noticed. They were too busy talking to each other. They started taking their lunches together. And it wasn't long before they began taking short walks into the woods during their lunch break. In the forest Micah somehow grew even more chatty.

"I can't wait for the winter," he said during one of these excursions. "People don't like the cold. But I don't mind it. I like it. I like how the sun can shine right on you but is still cold. People prefer trees when they have leaves. But I also like the trees without leaves. I might like them even more. I like how you can see better without the leaves. You can see more of the forest. More of the sky. The cold sunshine, the early sunsets. And then, when the leaves come back, and the sun stays out longer and warms up, it feels like something new. Like a miracle in a way. You can't have spring unless you have winter. It just doesn't make sense to choose which season is nicest because you have to take them together. They're all—"

"Micah, *shhhhh.*" Rose whispered, with her index finger over her mouth. She pointed up at a gigantic bird perched high in one of the trees. It had to be a bird. But it didn't look like a bird up there. It looked like the silhouette of a large, hunched cat.

"A great horned," Micah whispered back.

"A great . . . *horn?*"

"A great horned owl," Micah said. "They like winter, too. Come here in the winter, and you'll be able to see it even better. That's what I mean about winter. . . ."

But he caught himself. He shut his mouth. And he let the moment pass in silence. In a shared silence. Together they watched the large bird. And Micah did his best not to let Rose know that he was more interested in watching her than the bird. But she knew. She knew he was stealing glances at her. And she did her best, too, to not let him know that she knew. And did her best to fight the urge to take Micah's hand.

During these walks, while Micah chatted away, Rose would occupy herself by picking mushrooms. She had been reading as much as she could about foraging, about which mushrooms and berries and greenery were safe to eat. Mushrooms were her favorite. At first, she would collect everything she'd harvested and save them for day trips into town, where she would show her harvest to an Amish woman who worked at the grocery store. After a conversation in the produce aisle, the woman had encouraged Rose and given her things to read on the subject. She was always happy to sort through Rose's mushrooms, to make sure she'd picked the right kind. The first few times she'd done this, the woman had picked out a small pile of inedible mushrooms. Each week Rose made progress.

"Perfect!" the old woman said to Rose one week, handing back her sack of mushrooms. "Let's see you do it a few more times."

And she did. The next few rounds were all the same: perfect scores. Her mushroom professor told her that she was a "certified forager" and gave her a little handmade mushroom patch, which Rose immediately sewed onto her harvesting sack.

None of this, however, was told to Micah. Instead, during their walks, Rose would simply harvest a few choice mushrooms off the forest floor, then hold one out to Micah.

"Try it," she said with a little grin.

He just shook his head.

"They're tastiest when they're freshly picked."

Micah looked at her, uncharacteristically at a loss for words. He didn't dare touch the mushroom, much less eat it.

"What?" she said. "You don't *trust* me?"

She popped a mushroom into her mouth and ate it rapidly. Then stared at him, with widening eyes, and acted as if she was suddenly choking. And then immediately relented and let him off the hook.

"You think *my* face looked bad?" she said. "You should have seen *your* face!"

"I knew you were joking."

"No, you didn't," she said. "You were scared. I saw it. You thought I was gonna die right here. *Admit it*. You thought you were gonna lose me forever."

They always stayed out too long. And it was always his fault. But in Micah's monologues, Rose heard something special. Something that made her stop and pay attention. Even when he was pattering on about something mundane, his unusual perspective came through, strong and soulful. Even when he was talking about furniture, he somehow found a way to move her.

"In my eyes, if it's got a top and steady legs, that doesn't mean it's *a table*," Micah told her once as they walked through the woods. "It isn't a table until it's *beautiful*."

She'd stopped for a moment when he'd said that and looked at him. She saw in his face that he wasn't trying to be clever. He was just being sincere. And, in that moment, she had to work hard to prevent herself from saying, "Micah, *you're* beautiful."

Chapter Five

April liked to clean the house when everybody was out. One afternoon she came across a three-subject spiral notebook under some books on Rose's bedstand. Her first thought was nothing more than a pang of nostalgia. For a moment, the sight took her back to high school. She continued sweeping. But when she crouched down to sweep under Rose's bed, she saw three more spiral notebooks stacked one on top of the other. And they, too, were thick, three-subject notebooks, and worn. She grabbed one. Then hesitated. These belonged to Rose. She knew that. And she knew, too, the feeling of having her privacy invaded. Her mother used to read her diaries. For years. She didn't know about it, until one day, in high school, her mother had gotten particularly drunk and began quoting passages from it, in front of her friends. She'd promised herself, right there, never to read someone's diary. And as an older sister she had had plenty of opportunities. But she'd never opened up Rose's private diaries. And she wasn't going to start now.

So she continued sweeping. She carefully dusted the

notebooks, moved them aside, and swept behind them. Then she finished cleaning the rest of the room and went downstairs to make some lunch for herself and the others, as she did every day. The others, however, were still out. Rose was helping Joseph and his brother bring some produce and canned goods—including some of Rose's jams—to a farmer's market in Lancaster. They would be out all day.

April sliced some bread and spread some cream cheese and tomato on it. She thought about her sister, and the last few weeks. Rose had been acting pretty strangely, even by the new standards set by Rose's post-kidnapping strangeness. Occasionally she would say things that simply made no sense to April. A few days earlier, they had been sitting on the porch together, drinking lemonade, and Rose suddenly got up and said, "I don't like to sit here." April didn't like to challenge Rose these days, and she generally went along with Rose's moods. Whatever Rose wanted, April was fine with it. But she was confused by this announcement.

"You mean you don't want to sit here *now*," April had replied, "or you . . . never like to sit here?"

Rose didn't reply right away. Then finally she said, "Never."

"Why?" April asked very carefully, knowing that asking such questions was often not helpful to her sister.

"Because," Rose said, "see those trees over there?" She pointed to the twin willows that stood at the edge of the cornfield, right next to the path that Joseph had made into the woods. "I don't like them," Rose said. Then added: "And they don't like me."

And that was that. Rose walked off. April was left sitting there alone, looking at the willows and wondering what on earth her sister might have meant by her words.

Now, as April ate her lunch and thought about her sister's odd behavior, she also recalled something else. Now that she was thinking about it, she had read something of Rose's diaries. When Rose was missing, April had looked at some of Rose's writings. She'd forgotten about that, just as she had forgotten about a lot that had to do with Rose's disappearance. But now she remembered. She had been cleaning up Rose's stuff, getting it ready for storage. It was a particularly tough thing to do because it had meant that she was giving up hope of finding her sister. At the time, her friends assured her that it wasn't about giving up hope. That it was just a practical measure—so that she could stop paying rent for the empty room—and that as soon as Rose was found, they would simply get her a new place.

And, of course, they turned out to be right. As it turned out, reading those diaries had yielded some critical information about Rose. Information that helped April in the search for her missing sister. It hadn't felt like an invasion of Rose's privacy at all. In fact, Rose had left April a note, assuming that she'd see it in exactly that circumstance: if something happened to her. It had been essential, in that instance, that April read the diary. Maybe that was still true today. Was it possible? Was it possible that reading this diary wasn't just an act of snooping but a means of helping Rose, of accessing some part of her that was otherwise hidden to view, a part that needed to be seen?

Hadn't Rose left the notebooks out in easy view? She knew that April cleaned in there. She knew April would see them. Maybe she *wanted* her to read them.

Did Rose want April to know her inner thoughts? April had noticed that her sister had grown closer to Micah. She noticed how Rose brought his name up a lot. She saw them go off together on long walks. What did they discuss out there, in the woods? What was Rose telling *him?* Given what April herself had overheard—or, she could admit, eavesdropped—of their conversations, Rose was opening up to this man.

Small gestures hinted at large changes. Or so it seemed to April. On a suddenly chilly evening, she'd witnessed Rose graze her hand over Micah's wrist and say, "Hey, could you run inside and grab my scarf? It's hanging by the door." Without a word, he'd put down the saw he was using, and trotted toward the house. It was the smallest thing, the smallest intimacy. The kind that says so much.

If this new, strange man was given access to Rose's mind, certainly her own sister should be equally as trusted. If there was something urgent, something that April needed to know, she wanted to know it.

April knew that she was being nosy. She knew she was justifying her decision in her own head. And she also didn't care. Maybe that, too, was happening for a reason. In the past year and half, during Rose's disappearance, April had learned to trust her judgment, to trust her instincts. And her instincts were telling her to open up these notebooks.

April left her sandwich half-eaten on the table. She

went and sat on the floor of Rose's room, with the most recent notebook open on her lap.

I saw him again today.

She checked the date on the entry. It was from two weeks ago. She took a deep breath and continued reading.

I saw him again today. Yes, again. Because I saw him a bunch of weeks ago. Also, a bunch of months ago. Yes, now that I write this, I can say for sure that I have seen him now three times since I moved into this house. He knows where I am. He watches me. Every time . . .

April heard someone knock on the front door. It was someone from Joseph's work crew. They had a question for her. She quickly closed the notebook, slid it back into its place on the nightstand, and left the room.

Rose was in town that day, tagging along on chores with Joseph, mostly in the hope of running into Micah at the grocery store, as they often did when they went in on Fridays. And she was not disappointed. As usual, Micah was accompanied by his niece, Becca, who'd started to take a liking to Rose in the weeks since they'd first met.

"So are you gonna *come?*" Becca was asking her as she pulled on Rose's sleeve.

"Your birthday isn't for months, Beck," Micah said to the girl. "Don't be a pest."

"And anyway," Rose said, "I'm not sure whether I'm invited . . . it's probably just for family." Rose spoke directly to the girl and tried not catch the eye of Micah.

"No, no!" Becca said, pulling harder on her sleeve. "It's not just for family! Rachel is gonna be there—she's gonna make a pie. She's not family! Least not yet!"

"Who's Rachel?" Rose asked. Rose, still trying to avoid Micah's eyes, sensed some rapid movement from his direction. Some shifting. She dared not look.

"Oh, you *gotta* meet Rachel!" Becca said. "Micah and Rachel are getting *married!*"

Now, despite herself, Rose quickly turned to Micah. She couldn't help it. She knew she was giving herself away, but she didn't care. She needed to see his reaction. For once, he wasn't looking at her. No, he was looking at the ground.

Rose turned back to Becca and placed her hand gently on the little girl's head.

"Oh, how fun," she said to the child. "And I had *no* idea."

And then—despite herself, once again—she turned back to Micah, who hadn't moved or, from appearances, even breathed or blinked in the last few seconds.

That night Rose skipped out on the nightly ritual in the house. She and April would usually cook together. Then the three of them, Rose, April and Joseph, and often one of Joseph's family or friends, would eat together. Afterward, Joseph would clean up and wash the dishes while April and Rose sat in the living room, chatting, drawing, playing a board game, or working on one of their small

side projects, such as making jewelry for Rose's Etsy
store. But that night she skipped all of it. And holed herself up in her room.

"Is she okay?" Joseph whispered to April.

"She's fine," April said.

But she was also concerned. And during dinner she
drifted upstairs and knocked on Rose's door. She heard
Rose's voice, muffled and listless, telling her to come in.
She could tell that Rose had been crying. She was lying
in bed, curled up on her side, scrolling through her phone
continuously and expressionlessly.

"What's up?" Rose said.

"What's up with *you?*" April replied.

"Just not feeling up to it tonight."

A slight, unspoken awkwardness had developed between the sisters. April was living an Amish life now, em-
bracing the clothing and customs, and (slowly, cautiously)
being embraced more by the community, too. She was
working hard to learn how to speak Pennsylvania Dutch,
and her progress was going a long way toward gaining
the trust of her new community, her new family. She was
even talking about putting her newfound knowledge of
Amish cookery to work in the restaurant she was busy
trying to launch.

Rose was not on that path. She respected the Amish
ways and customs, but she was very much a visitor there.
She hitched rides to town partly because she wanted to
charge her phone in the café, and would hoard that battery
life for the next few days until she could recharge it again.
Sometimes Rose would look at her sister from across the
room and she would see an Amish woman who was not

familiar to her. And sometimes April would look at Rose and see a part of herself that was too familiar, a former life in Philly she was trying to put behind her.

Even if April didn't expect her sister to join the community in the way she had, it was sometimes hard for her to switch back and forth between the world of her sister and her new world. But April was keen to give Rose space. And taking a break from the usual for one night was a perfectly understandable thing to do. Also, April sensed something. She knew her sister.

"Is something . . . bothering you, though?"

Rose scrolled more, her eyes glued to the screen. Then she stopped. And dropped the phone down on her bed.

"It's too stupid to even say, Ri," Rose said.

"C'mon, babe, it's me," April said, sitting on her sister's bed. "You can tell me anything."

"I didn't expect to be so . . . upset, I guess? To find out that Micah's engaged. Like, what did I expect? Seriously? And who cares anyway?"

"Oh," April said.

"And it's just thrown open this door to everything. Sadness and anger, and then, like, more anger at being angry, and then embarrassment for feeling angry. I feel like I'm a kid again. I feel so silly for admitting that I was, I don't know, secretly having these silly thoughts."

Tears welled up in Rose's eyes.

"I mean, I feel betrayed. Like he lied to me. Like *everyone* lied to me. And then I feel crazy for thinking that. Literally crazy. Maybe I'm losing my mind, losing my grip on reality for thinking things like this."

"You're *not* crazy," April said. "Look at me, Rose.

You're not losing a grip on anything, okay? These are normal feelings."

"Yeah, but I'm not normal, Ri. We both know that," she said. "And I don't want to be feeling like this."

"I know, I know," she said, scooting closer on the bed and taking her sister's hand. "It's the worst. But this thing . . . it really is normal to feel this. We've all been there. You *know* I have. I know it's a very different situation, but do you remember Knuckle-Tattoo Tommy?"

Rose, for a moment, forgot her tears and laughed.

"Omigod, how could I forget? The guy who didn't know how to tie his shoes?"

"Yup, that guy. The worst part of it isn't that it doesn't work out, but that you're left feeling like a complete idiot when you realize how completely impossible it was, and how this was totally obvious to everyone, right away. Everyone but you."

"Did you know Micah was engaged?" Rose said, a sudden fierceness in her voice. She dropped April's hand, and gave her a look that startled April and sent a tingle down her spine. There were moments, like this one, when Rose scared April a bit.

"I didn't know. But you know I would have told you everything, if I'd had any clue. You *know* that, little sis. Nobody's got your back like me."

April picked up Rose's hand and squeezed it.

"I know, I know," Rose murmured.

"Listen, Rosie," April said, pulling her sister in for a hug, "I'll keep that guy away from here. And I'll make up an excuse. I won't tell him the reason why. You don't need to worry about this, okay?"

Rose didn't reply. But April could feel her crying quietly into her shoulder.

As the weeks went by, Rose felt more and more comfortable on the farm, buffeted by her routines. Days would go by without any intrusive thoughts and feelings. She was, for the first time in a long time, feeling like a normal person.

On most days, Rose was out and about. In the fields, in the forest, foraging, or helping Joseph build the new shed he was working on, or going to town on an errand. But on this particular day, she decided to give herself one of her days off to just laze about the house. She would take catnaps and long showers, and recline in bed reading one of the new novels she picked up on their monthly trip to Target, something by Shelley Laurenston or Alyssa Cole or Charlotte Hubbard.

This alone time, she was beginning to realize, was also necessary to her sanity. Without it, she found herself angry and lashing out at April and Joseph, barely able to tolerate even the slightest demand they put on her time. At some point it occurred to her that she was angry because she blamed them for depriving her of a world, a mental space, that was hers alone. So she and April would orchestrate these days off—at first, April was wary of leaving Rose all alone, and she would even take shifts with Joseph, staying close by to watch the house from afar. But after a while, when things had started to feel more normal and secure, April felt comfortable venturing off and leaving Rose alone.

And it helped that these days off seemed to be doing the trick. At the end of a day alone Rose would feel refreshed and was even excited to see other people. When April and Joseph would return in the early evening to eat dinner, she was friendly and warm, her moodiness forgotten.

On one of these afternoons alone, Rose was up in her room. She had just woken up from a nap. It was a short nap but she felt as though her brain had gotten a deep tissue massage. She woke up alert and calm and feeling strong. She made herself some tea with milk, stretched, and got cozy with her new novel, which was just starting to get really good. Out of the corner of her eye she noticed something. Some movement. She paused and lifted her head. Now she could also hear something.

She went to her window. A man. An old man, it seemed, or someone weathered and injured, was limping across the lawn behind the barn. Rose dropped to her knees to stay out of sight. She wanted to pull the curtain but was afraid he might see the movement. So she crouched by the corner of her window and peeked out. The man was in tattered clothes and old beat-up work boots. Even though the weather was too warm for it, he wore a Carhartt jacket, which seemed to have been dredged up from the bottom of a river. He had a pronounced limp in his left leg and a long scraggly beard. Bizarrely—or so it seemed to Rose— he lugged a midsized rolling suitcase.

He walked hunched over. And since he walked facing the ground, there was no chance he would look up and see her in the window. Rose watched him carefully.

Finally he arrived at the house. Rose could hear his

heavy steps on the stairs to the house, each one landing with a decisive thump, like a large sack of flour. Then there was a knock on the door. Louder, sharper, stronger than she expected. As she'd watched him advance toward the house, she'd weighed in her mind the question of whether to answer the door or not. Watching the limping, raggedly dressed man, she decided to answer it. The man clearly needed some food or water.

But something in the way he knocked on the door, the sharpness of the sound, turned her mind in the other direction. She decided not to answer the door. She felt it was the right decision, though she felt bad about it, too. What if this man was desperate? She listened for a while as the man knocked. Then he cursed a bit. And spat. And eventually she heard the heavy steps again, dropping on the stairs in the other direction. She watched as the man dragged himself back in the direction he'd come from and eventually disappeared onto the main road.

That night at dinner, Rose was unusually talkative. Her day off had gone very well, and she felt ready to chat and be social. She was halfway through a story about Darlene, the dog, about her attempts to climb a tree the way she'd seen a cat do. There was a knock at the door. Rose immediately stopped her story. She stared at the door. April, who was sitting across from Rose, hadn't heard the knock and wondered why Rose had suddenly stopped. Joseph, who was puttering around the kitchen, close to the front door, had also heard the knock. And he had, without much thought, thrown his hand towel down on the counter, and gone to answer.

When the door opened, the old man, the man Rose had seen earlier in the day, was standing there. She froze.

"Sorry to bother you good people," the man said in a raspy voice.

It would have been almost impossible to hear him except that Rose and April, who had now turned back to see what was happening, were both silent and staring.

"I don't have nowhere to go," he said. "If you got some food to spare . . ."

"Come in," Joseph said.

April shot him a look. Which Joseph was trying to ignore.

Then April turned to Rose, shrugged and mouthed *Sorry*.

"We're seated for supper," Joseph was now saying. "We have plenty to share, friend. Would you like to have something to eat . . . ?"

"Or maybe some food *to go?*" April said. "We can pack up something nice for the road, Joseph."

Now Joseph gave her a surprised look.

"You can sit by the fire and warm yourself up," Joseph said to him. "I'll bring you something to eat. Once you've had some food, maybe you will tell us a little bit about yourself."

April was losing patience.

"*Joseph,*" April said. Joseph ignored her.

"And then," Joseph said to the stranger, taking his suitcase and helping him remove his coat, "when you are done, we will find you a place to lie down for the night."

"Joseph!" April said. "Can I *talk* to you for moment? Right now."

April got up, ready to march over to Joseph and pull him aside. But Rose tugged her back gently.

"It's okay, Ri," Rose said.

"No, it's not," April replied.

"No, it is. Seriously. We're not going to send this man out there into the night."

April threw her head back.

"*Ugh*. The two of you, I swear! Fine. Guess this saves me from having to make breakfast tomorrow since we'll all be hacked to death by then anyway."

Joseph shot her yet another look. And Rose said, "April, c'mon . . ."

"I'm sorry to be such a bother," the old man said meekly.

Now both Rose and Joseph gave April looks. April just sighed.

"It's not a bother," Joseph said. "I'm glad you're here. I'm glad you found us."

"Because I can go," the old man said.

"No, no, stay," Joseph said. "My wife is from the city, where the customs are different."

"*Customs,*" April said with a snorting laugh. "Hey, Rosie, I feel like in Philly we had a different word for it."

The old man ate quietly. April watched him carefully. She was surprised by his manners. Despite his appearance—and a closer look revealed just how ragged his clothes were—his table manners were meticulous and dignified, even though it was obvious how hungry he was.

Rose was also watching the man carefully. She knew it was him. She knew it was Whitey. His disguise was so thin, she thought, *he must* want *me to know it's him.* A part of her was terrified but that part felt deeply buried, passive. The active part of her was just curious: Why? Why would he return in this way? She knew she would have to tell April and Joseph who this was. But for some reason she decided it could wait. It must wait. In the meantime she sat utterly silent. She didn't think she would be able to speak even if called upon. But she watched and watched. She watched how careful he was not to make eye contact with her. Except once, when he just started to look her way, then quickly turned back to his plate instead.

The man finished his heaping portion of chicken and potatoes and waved off an offer of seconds. April jumped up to bring out some fruit and tea for dessert.

"Tell me, friend, what is your name?" Joseph said as he gathered up the dinner plates and cleared the table. "Where do you come from?"

"Well," the man replied, "my name is the easy part, I guess. It's Samuel. People call me Sam."

Now he turned to Rose and looked directly at her. She immediately turned away.

"Where I come from," he continued. "Well, that's harder to say, isn't it? Was born over by Wisconsin. But traveled around a bit. Spent a lot time down by St. Louis. But that was some time ago. These days I spend most of my time back around here. Got some people 'round about. You're probably wondering why I'm not staying with them. Well, that would be another story."

April could detect a slight Amish accent. Joseph must have been thinking it, too, because he asked his next question in Pennsylvania Dutch.

"I'd prefer not to say," the man replied in English. "Don't think they'd want me to name 'em."

And when Joseph continued in Pennsylvania Dutch, the man quickly cut in.

"I prefer English," he said, "if that's okay with you. I understand okay, but it's easier for me to speak in English."

"Of course," Joseph said.

When Rose sensed that the stranger had turned his gaze back to her, she realized suddenly that she was staring down at the ground, almost unable to lift her head. April also seemed to notice this because she put a hand on Rose's back and began to gently caress her.

"Okay, then," April said. "Rose and I will go and fix you a place to sleep. You must be very tired."

Upstairs, April rummaged through the linen closet looking for a spare pillowcase. When she found it, she grabbed it and set it on top of the rest of the bedding, then pulled her sister into Rose's room, steered her to sit on the bed, and closed the door behind her.

"Okay," she said, joining Rose on the bed, "what's going on in that head of yours?"

Rose made no reply.

"Talk to me, Rosie," April said. "Just give me the word, and this weirdo is out of here. Joe is right. We do things differently in Philly. In Philly, this rando would be turned out by now."

"We're not in Philly anymore," Rose said.

"I'm always in Philly," April said.

"He seems harmless."

"*Seems* is the key word."

"It's fine, Ri."

"He can sleep in the shed. We'll give him a sleeping bag. He'll be fine out there."

Rose shook her head slowly. "It's not right," she said.

"Okay, but I'm getting the sense that you're low-key freaking out here. Am I imagining that?"

Rose pursed her lips for a moment. Her mind took her to that first moment when the man walked into the house, when Rose saw him and knew, without a doubt, that it was Whitey. She knew by the chill in her bones, the way her joints locked.

"I'm not *freaking* out, Ri. I'm not some mess that constantly needs to be mopped up."

"Hey, babe, I'm sorry. I didn't mean it like that. You just seem . . . really uncomfortable. I mean, *I am, too.* Nobody should feel that way in their own house."

"Is this *my* house?" Rose said, looking up at April.

"Umm, *yes*, Rosie. This is totally your house," April said. "C'mon, you *know* that."

"I know, I know," Rose said.

She looked up, suddenly, and gave April the most resolute look she could muster. She nodded decisively and said, "Okay, I'm fine. I really am, Ri. I'm fine. And I'm not gonna let this mess with me."

"Okay," April said, taking Rose's hand. "Old Man Winter will sleep on the couch, I guess. Tomorrow morning we'll give him a nice farm breakfast and then he's *out*. And we go on with our lives. Sound good?"

"Yup," Rose said.

"Do you want me to sleep in your bed with you tonight?"

Rose shook her head.

"Okay, Rosie. But if you change your mind, lemme know. For now, just go to your room and chill for the night, 'kay? You don't need to deal with this anymore. I'll take care of the rest."

April squeezed Rose's hand, grabbed the bedding, and disappeared through the door, leaving Rose sitting on the bed alone.

That night Rose lay in her bed, wide awake. She was annoyed with herself for not having had the courage to look at the man—at Whitey—when he'd turned to her. She should have mustered up the strength to look into his eyes. It was her best chance to size up his motives. What was he after? Why had he come here? Did he really think Rose wouldn't recognize him? One thing was certain. If he'd bet on her silence, he was right.

But why was she so silent? Why hadn't she told anyone it was him? Why was she . . . okay with his presence? Why had she been so weirdly calm about this sudden incursion? As Rose turned in her bed and mulled these thoughts over, she realized that her own motives were as mysterious to her right now as Whitey's. It had been hours since she'd heard Joseph and April going to their bedroom. And then the house had grown silent.

A quiet voice within Rose; a voice that was always there in the background suddenly spoke clearly. *Rose,* it said, *you are in danger. Rose, do something. Rose,* now.

Somebody seemed to be shaking her. *Do something. Do something.*

She sprang up. Suddenly she was awake. Whitey was in this house. This wasn't the time for her strange, complex psychological fantasies. This wasn't a gray area. This was a man who had almost murdered her. He'd found her again. He was back. He was only feet away from her in this dark, quiet house. Why had he come? Why else? He'd come for her. To harm her.

And what if he hadn't come to harm her? What if he was just being a creep and trying to spy on her? Even so, the next time, or the time after that, he would come back, and he would harm her. Tonight she had an opportunity to be rid of this menace for good.

She sprang into action. There was a knife in a box under her bed. It was a Timber Rattler full tang bowie knife with an 11 3/8 inch-long steel blade. A hardwood handle. She'd purchased it on a Walmart errand one day. While April was busy buying yarn, she'd drifted over to the camping and sporting goods department. When the salesclerk asked her what kind of knife she wanted she'd said "a long one." She didn't know anything about knives and hadn't been prepared to purchase one. It was a whim. Based on a series of bad premonitions she'd been having. The salesclerk had asked, "What do you need it for?" Without hesitating she'd said, "Self-defense." She seemed to detect a surprised look from him but couldn't quite tell. And frankly didn't much care. He'd presented her with the Timber Rattler bowie, and she'd liked the look of it. And liked the feel. It had some weight to it. But it wasn't heavy. She bought it right there, slipped it into her backpack, and didn't tell April about it. On a few occasions, she'd taken it out of its box and held it up. Run her finger along its length. She made a point of always carrying it with her, when she went out into the forest alone. A few times, she'd taken it out and used it to harvest mushrooms, amazed at its razor sharpness.

She reached under her bed and grabbed it. She placed

it, safely buttoned into its sheath, under her pillow. She practiced pulling it out. She would unbutton it while it was still under the pillow, then, in one quick motion, pull it out and brandish it at her attacker. Low, at his legs, at his crotch. She'd watched some YouTube videos about using a knife for self-defense. She'd practiced what she'd learned. She lay with the knife under her pillow for a while. There was no danger of her falling asleep tonight. She flipped on the lamp on her bedstand.

Then the voice came to her. Her own voice. *Rose, he's in the house. The time for self-defense is past. Don't wait. Strike first, strike last. End this now.*

There was no doubt in her mind that she needed to kill Whitey tonight. The question wasn't whether it was justified, or whether she would go to jail. The only question was if she had the guts. And also, how likely was it that she would end up getting hurt or worse if she attacked first?

Rose snapped the knife out of its harness. She began to walk toward her door, with the naked knife in hand. It felt strange and dangerous to walk around the house with it unsheathed. She decided to walk around the room a bit, to get used to it, to holding it at her side, with its point facing the floor. But then she decided that all this walking was making too much noise. Someone would be woken up by it. So she stopped. She tiptoed to the door, which was closed. Then she listened.

The house was very still. She faintly heard the sound of Joseph, quietly and regularly snoring. She also heard the man downstairs. He was shifting around. Was he walking? Were those his feet on the floor? She listened more.

No. He was not walking. He was shifting on the couch. He was lying down. She waited. Her ears adjusted to the deep country silence. She could faintly hear him breathing. He seemed asleep. This was her chance to kill Whitey. Would anyone fault her for it? It wasn't merely vengeance. It *was* self-defense. He was in her house. Why was he here? Nobody would blame her for doing what she knew, without a shadow of a doubt, that she must now do.

Chapter Six

"It's your turn to babysit Mom," April said, as she gave her face one last look in the mirror next to the door. She checked her mascara: no crumbly bits. Checked her teeth: no lipstick.

"It's always my turn," Rose said.

"Only at night," April said. "And on weekends."

"It's not *fair!*"

"I'm in high school, Rosie," April said. "I get to go out, okay? And if I stayed here, where would you even go? Like, to get slushies at 7-Eleven with Katie?"

"Well, yeah, maybe," Rose said. "So?"

April rolled her eyes.

"But that's not what I mean," Rose said.

April opened the door and took a step into the hall. But then she stopped, turned around, and stepped back into the doorway.

"Well," she said with a sigh. "What do you mean?"

"I mean, why don't you ever stay home anymore? Why can't we *both* be here, like we used to?"

"Oh, Rosie," April said. "Don't make me sad right now, okay?"

She quickly touched up her mascara with her pinkie, closed the door, and was off. Maybe Rose would see her in the morning, straggling in, her club clothes falling off her body as if suddenly made of thin paper. Or maybe she wouldn't see her at all until the evening.

And that's how it was in those days. April was becoming more independent and Rose, it seemed, more chained to a mother who was drinking herself to death. The woman who lived in the corner of their studio apartment, sitting on the bed with a bottle balanced between her knees, with her back propped up against the wall, seemed to be shrinking, even as Rose was growing. In Rose's mind, these things were directly connected, as though all the mass that her mother's body seemed to be shedding was actually just transferred to her own small form. Her body felt monstrous for this reason, as if she was cannibalizing her mom. Or sometimes, as if they were merging, sinking together.

Rose had read that a person who is drowning usually makes almost no sound, often doesn't even cause a ripple in the water. *It's not like in the movies,* she'd read, where the drowning victim thrashes and shouts for help. No, in reality, from the outside, the person drowning can be observed almost placidly floating, suspended right below the surface. Sometimes their motion, if there is any at all, is described as *climbing a ladder to nowhere,* she'd read.

April was watching this happen to Rose and doing nothing. And then, it seemed, even that had changed: April wasn't even watching anymore. She was too busy with other things. She'd stopped paying attention, and the world hadn't ended when she'd stopped watching. Their mother didn't die immediately.

April said she'd more than paid her dues. So now that Rose was a bit older, it was her turn to help out a bit. Her turn to be responsible, to carry more of the burden. April said Rose could handle this. It would even do her some good.

And Rose was handling it. At a great cost. Her grades plummeted. She was missing more and more days of school. And the more she missed, the less she felt that going in was worth it. The idea of sticking it out for another two years, so that she could start high school began to seem impossible. She could barely get to the end of each week. Watching her mom. Buying food, making food. Washing the dishes. Doing laundry. Cleaning the apartment. She felt like Cinderella. But with no one, and certainly no fairy godmother, there to pull her out of her servitude.

Buying the food was easier than the other shopping task, the all-important shopping run, which she, as a minor, couldn't do herself. So she would have to help clothe her mom, then drag her three blocks to the liquor store, so that she could buy the bottles that kept her alive, and made all of their lives miserable. Rose had already made the mistake, which she would never, ever repeat, of trying to cut her mother off from drink, which led first to a whirlwind of violent abuse, and then, when Rose had held firm, to a terrifying bout of withdrawal characterized by waves of quaking and vomiting that Rose was certain would kill her.

Meanwhile, April withdrew into her own world even more. The more time April spent out with her friends, the deeper she got into pills, into drinking. *You're just like her,* Rose wanted to tell April. *You're just like Mom.*

You're gonna end up like her. But she never dared say it
to her sister. As April would get ready to go out, or as she
would shuffle back in, zombielike, smelling like death,
sometimes after an absence of days, Rose would glare
at her, certain that her angry eyes would convey this
message. *You're just like Mom.* Or, more precisely: *Please
stop being like Mom. Don't abandon me. I need you.*

Though she hadn't worked up the courage to say it,
some part of her believed that April was getting the message just through those looks. But this was a fantasy. And
Rose, even at her young age, knew that. She knew that
April wasn't actually getting her message, wasn't getting
any messages, in fact. In the past—and not long ago, but
how long just a few months seemed!—April and Rose
could communicate like this, nonverbally. All it took was
a look, or some small gesture of the hands, and the sisters
could tell each other anything. But that line of communication was dead now. April was somewhere else, and
unreachable. Rose wasn't really afraid of telling April,
Please don't be like Mom. Please come back to me. She
wasn't afraid of how April might react. No, she was afraid
there would be no reaction at all. Just a dead stare. And
then she would know, with certainty, that her sister really
was just like their mother. That was what scared her.

The night of the accident, April was, of course, nowhere
to be found. Maybe she was at the club. Maybe she was
with her boyfriend. Maybe she was somewhere with her
friends. She would be the last to have remembered where
she might have been that night. Rose, on the other hand,
knew exactly where she herself had been: she'd gone to
7-Eleven, just as April had teased her. But it was one of

the few places where seventh graders could go at night, and it just happened to be located a few blocks from her home and from a few of her friends. They'd gone there and walked up and down the aisles as the store manager kept a close eye on them. And once they bought their candy and drinks, they went behind the store, where someone—they never did find out who—had set out a couch, which had become disgusting through all the waves of weather and urban nastiness. But to the kids it was freedom. They'd sit on the couch listening to music, eating their junk food, and making each other laugh. And they did it for hours. Until one of them had to go home, and the spell was broken. Or until some adult, a cop or the 7-Eleven store manager or some pervert came by and forced them out. But sometimes they could be out there late into the night.

Earlier that evening, Rose had been unsure if she was going to go out at all. Her mother didn't seem well. She could barely get out of bed. April was gone. Rose couldn't even remember the last time she'd seen her around. She'd fixed her mom some mac and cheese. They'd just made a run to the liquor store. So she was fully stocked. Her mom was weak and could barely talk. But she was often that way, especially as it got later into the night. She would sit in front of the TV, watching blankly, barely moving at all. Rose could never tell if she was asleep. But at some point she would slump a bit, and Rose would go to her, nudge her awake, and pull her toward the bathroom to get ready for bed.

She did that again this night. Because she'd done it so many other times before, she was hyperaware of the small changes in her mom. On this night she seemed slower, heavier. Less responsive. But eventually she got herself up from her chair, as she did every night. She got herself into the bathroom, into bed. Once there, Rose had a decision to make: stay home or go out with her friends. She drifted over to her mom's bed. She could hear the sounds of her sleeping, the labored breathing, the low moan. The occasional coughing fit. But other than that, her mother seemed deeply asleep. If anything, she slept more placidly than usual. If Rose knew better, if she were older and wiser, or at least more experienced, she might have put it together. Might have seen this calm for what it was: a warning sign.

Later, when they pumped her stomach, the ER techs found a variety of pills in her stomach. But Rose didn't know about that. There was no reason for her to think that her mother's drinking that night was anything unusual. She drank, as always, constantly. She drank until she was barely able to stand. But she didn't seem drunk. True alcoholics rarely do. There was no particular fear that her mother would vomit. It happened sometimes. But it was rare. And when it happened, it was uneventful. But this night was different. She'd popped a bunch of pills. Who knew why? Was she trying to kill herself? Was she just sloppy? Rose suspected the second. She imagined her mother, somehow getting her hands on these pills— maybe from someone in the building—and just popping them all into her mouth right away, all at once, without even noticing. A minute later she'd probably not even remember that she'd swallowed them. That was how she was. Impulsive, living minute to minute. Acting instinctually. The kind of addict who popped whatever came into her hand. It was hard for Rose to imagine that her mother might be organized enough, reflective enough, to intentionally plan and execute a suicide. But there was no real way to know. Because Rose also knew that her mom was the kind of person who, even if she did try to kill herself, was impaired enough to actually forget that she'd done so.

Her intentions that night were, in any case, irrelevant. The pills and bottomless beers and vodka had put her into a stupor that was deeper than her usual numbness. It was a combination that could have been, on its own, enough to kill her. And it was certainly enough to render her nearly comatose. She had made no effort to get up. From what Rose—who found her—and the medics could tell, she'd barely even moved when she'd vomited. When Rose had gotten home, she knew something was wrong the moment she'd walked into the studio.

The place reeked. She knew instantly that her mother had vomited. Her first reaction, however, was annoyance, and of course, disgust. She didn't, at first, quite grasp the danger that the vomiting posed. Even so, she didn't waste time. She went directly to her mother and saw the mess. Saw it all over the pillow and on the left side of her face. She was just lying there in a pool of it. Saw her lying still, not waking up. At that moment, she grasped just how bad the situation was.

As luck would have it, her mother had been lying on her side when it happened. Had she been on her back, the medics told her, she'd have died within minutes. But as it was, she was still breathing. The vomiting had, it seemed, happened only moments before Rose had returned. This, too, was dumb luck.

Rose recalled little from that night. A part of her was panicked. But she was oddly calm on the outside. She had been expecting that something like this might happen one day. She'd imagined it often, visualized almost every detail. Now that it was actually happening, it somehow didn't seem surprising at all. It felt obvious, inevitable. Even though Rose felt deep emotions for her mother, when the time came to feel something, she simply couldn't.

April did not make it to the hospital. At least not right away. Rose did everything she could to contact her. But she couldn't find her. Finally they spoke. Their mother had been in the hospital for two weeks. Even after it became clear that her mother would survive the over-dose, the asphyxiation, the bigger problem became her alcohol withdrawal symptoms. The hospital stay became a detox for her. And when she came out, she still moved more slowly than ever and still seemed distant. But she was more lucid and better nourished than she had been in years.

For a short while, a matter of a couple weeks, things at home were slightly better. But then the situation slipped back into the old patterns. And, in the end, things were worse because her mom, with the short period of detox undone, was now proving that she was beyond help.

April had refused to see how traumatizing this event had been to her twelve-year-old sister. She refused to ac-knowledge her own role in what had happened. Refused to help her sister deal with the fear and anxiety and guilt she had been feeling. Though neither of them had quite realized it at the time, a wedge had come between them. Neither sister had anyone in her life who was closer, in whom she could confide. And yet they could barely even look each other in the eye anymore.

It would be another five years, at least, until they had a real conversation again. April, in tears, apologized for everything. Apologized for abandoning her sister. Without even quite realizing it, she had herself been keeping a close account of all the ways she'd let Rose down, and now it all came out. Rose, also in tears, was just amazed.

"I didn't think you were paying attention to me at all during that time," she said.

"I was, I was," April said. "But that makes it worse, Rosie. I saw what was happening. I saw it all, but I didn't . . . I just couldn't . . ."

She broke down.

"I know, Ri. I know. I really, really do," Rose said. "I know you couldn't say anything. And I know why, too."

"You do?" April said, blowing her nose.

"Yes," Rose replied. "I know you couldn't say anything 'cause if you did, you'd get pulled back into . . . everything. And you couldn't do it. You were trying to save yourself. And the only way you knew how was to make a clean cut and go."

April sobbed.

"To make a clean cut and go . . . and leave you, leave my little sister . . ." April said, and began to cry again.

"Yes, you had to, though. You had to leave me. You didn't know how to save me. You were just trying to survive. You did your best."

"Oh, Rosie," April said, "I don't know if that's even true. I don't know if I was really doing my best. But I do want to do better now. I really want to."

It would still take another few years for them to build trust and to grow as close as they once had been. But after that happened, they were closer than ever. As they grew into adults they were so close, they hardly left each other's side—except, of course, for the long absence when Rose had been kidnapped. But even then, they remained close somehow spiritually. And when Rose returned—by something like a miracle—April had vowed to never let her sister out of her sight.

Chapter Seven

A burst of adrenaline suddenly coursed through Rose's veins. It came on so suddenly that she grabbed the door frame to restrain herself from throwing the door open, running downstairs, and jumping onto the couch where Whitey was sleeping, to shove this 11 3/8 inch-long steel blade directly into his neck.

It would work, her plan. She would have the element of surprise. It would be a matter of seconds. He would have a knife in him before he had a chance to open his eyes. Rose's mind was racing. Calculating the number of seconds, the number of steps her feet would have to take. It would be something like six to nine steps—two to the stairs, four down the stairs, then two to three to the couch. It would be a matter of three to four seconds. That's all it would take to put Whitey out of her life forever. Three to four seconds and she would be free.

Rose grew agitated. Her hand was shaking. This was no good. This was a problem. She needed to calm herself. She carefully put the knife down on the floor, next to her door. She was struggling hard not to crack open the door and make the dash. She knew that, even if it was the right thing to do, even if she was committed to her plan, she needed to think it through. Just a bit more.

First, there was the question of getting it right on the first try. There could be no errors. She needed to visualize the whole scenario so that she didn't encounter any surprises. She knew the steps downstairs and to the couch fairly well. But she needed to imagine taking them now, quickly and in the dark. There were no windows by the stairs, and she knew from past experience—previous bouts of insomnia, when she'd made her way downstairs to get a midnight snack—that those stairs could be very dark at night. The downstairs space, where Whitey was sleeping, was probably darker than usual because April had drawn the curtains to help him sleep better.

Rose needed to be able to see in the dark. She needed to let her eyes adjust to the darkness for a bit. She tiptoed to her bedstand now and turned off the light. She closed her blinds. She peeked outside and noticed that the moon had set. There was very little light coming in. For a moment, she thought about Micah. What would he think of this? What would he make of her, as a knife-wielding angel of vengeance? She couldn't help smiling at the thought. *If he can't handle blood what good is he, anyway?*

She had two options now. Either sneak downstairs, let her eyes adjust to the room and then, when she felt ready, pounce on the couch. Or she could just make a mad dash from her bedroom, down the stairs, and to the couch.

And then there was the question of stabbing him. She was certain she wanted to put the knife in his neck. It seemed the most efficient way to kill him. Stabbing him multiple times might be difficult to pull off. Better, she thought, one good piercing. The best spot, she figured, would be the side of his neck, where the jugular vein was. But what if he was sleeping on his belly? Was it worth stabbing whatever was exposed or should she try to turn him and then get that ideal angle? Turning him, of course, involved the risk of waking him and having him defend himself or simply move around, making his neck a harder target to hit. Even though every second meant more danger for her, it would probably be worth pausing to size up the target before striking.

Rose turned over each detail. She tried to visualize the assault and think of every possibility. As she did this, she made one big decision: she would sneak down the stairs quietly. To get as close as possible before attacking, to get her eyes and mind adjusted to the space. The risk was that she would wake him, or someone else in the house. But it was worth it. The key, she decided, was to move incredibly, incredibly slowly. An isolated creak of the floor every few minutes wouldn't wake anyone. Patience. Her body had become one giant beating heart. She felt almost lifted from the ground by adrenaline. Her hands couldn't stop moving. But she had to breathe, and control herself very carefully now, and be patient.

She now realized that she'd been waiting for this moment for a long time—many months. This was what she had been secretly planning for a long time—it was a plan so unlike her that she couldn't bring herself to admit it, much less to indulge it as a serious option. But the occasional fantasy she'd had of wanting Whitey to return, wanting to go to him . . . these thoughts, she now saw, weren't about wanting to be with him. Of course they weren't! They were about wanting to be close enough to him to put a blade in his neck. To free herself from him. Now that she was so close, she could barely wait a second longer. She could finally admit to herself that she was not just capable of killing this man, she was very much determined to put that plan into action.

She picked up the knife from the floor. She held it, blade tip facing behind her. Her hand was shaking. She took a few deliberate breaths. She practiced the stabbing motion. Her temptation was to take a big stab, to get force behind it. But that wasn't the best way. Because then she risked not hitting the right spot. Better, she decided, to make it a hard push, closer to the target, but then shift her full body weight into the knife. She felt around her own neck to find the spot she believed was the softest and most lethal. She practiced the death blow. She breathed again, and gently, ever so gently, turned her doorknob with her left hand, and pushed her door open.

She tiptoed toward the stairs. She did not walk down the stairs but sat down, leaning her weight against the wall, then slowly letting herself down one step at a time, in a sitting position, until she reached the bottom stair.

She was now crouching next to the front door. She could see the couch in the next room, just three or four steps away. She breathed. She listened. She opened her eyes wide, letting in whatever tiny light there was in the room. Her palm was so sweaty, she had to shift the knife into her left hand, to wipe her right palm on her nightshirt. She wiped the handle, as well. Then took it back into her right hand. Her grip on the handle was not as firm as she wanted it to be. She licked her hand, the way she'd seen baseball pitchers do to get a firmer grip on the ball. She breathed for a moment. The knife felt right in her hand again. She slowly came out of her crouch and stood. She could see Whitey on the couch. On his back. She could make out where his neck would be. She paid attention to her breath and leaned forward.

"Rose?" someone whispered. *"Rosie, is that you?"*

April was standing at the top of the stairs. Rose's heart dropped. She didn't answer. She held her breath. Maybe April was just going to the bathroom. Maybe she was groggy and would just go away.

"Rose!" April whispered, more insistently. *"What are you doing?"*

April tiptoed down a few steps and motioned for Rose to come back up the stairs.

"Be there in a second," Rose whispered back. And she quickly scampered to the kitchen and slid the knife under the sink, grabbed a cup and filled it with water, and tiptoed back upstairs. They both retreated into Rose's room.

"Everything all right?" April said, as she closed the door behind them. "It's like three in the morning."

"I couldn't sleep," Rose said.

"Yeah, I could hear," April said. "You were pacing around your room for almost an hour."

"Oh," Rose said. "Sorry. Didn't mean to wake you."

"I wasn't asleep. I'm not going to sleep with . . ." She gestured toward the door.

"Yeah, me neither."

"Oh, Rosie," April said, walking toward her and caressing her arm. "Omigod, you're *drenched* in sweat, you poor thing!"

"Ri," Rose said, "I have to tell you something."

"What, darling? What is it? You can tell me."

"I want to tell you why I was down there." April began to get nervous.

"Go on," she said.

"I was down there . . . to kill Whitey."

"*Whitey?* You were going to . . . kill . . . what are you saying?"

"That man is Whitey. He's in disguise. But I know it's him. And it's not a very good disguise because he wants me to know it's him."

"*Rose* . . ." April gave Rose a long look, and she seemed worried. "Rose . . . that man is not Whitey. And if he was—which he is *not*, but if he was—his disguise is actually *really* good. He looks nothing like him."

"Ri, it's him," Rose said. "I know what this man looks like. I know what it's like to be around him. . . . It's him. You only know him from photos."

April didn't respond. She gave her sister a long look, as if trying to size her up, judge her mental state.

"How were you going to . . . do it?"

"I have a bowie knife."

"Are you for real?"

"I bought it at Walmart."

April laughed.

"What are you talking about?"

"It's under the sink right now."

"Were you really going to use it on him?"

"Shouldn't I?"

"No, you absolutely should not."

"He doesn't belong in this house. I'm not going to wait to see what he does. I have a right to self-defense. Nobody is going to hold me responsible for defending myself against the man who kidnapped me."

"But, Rosie, it's *not* him."

Rose got very quiet and withdrew into herself.

"Are you going to stop me from doing this?" Rose said, crossing her arms.

"Yes," April said. "Rosie, *yes*. I'm going to stop you. This is a huge mistake. It would be the worst mistake you ever made. It would be the worst judgment call that *I've* ever made, and that's saying a lot."

Rose was silent. She looked down and refused to make eye contact with her sister.

"Rose, think about it: what if you're wrong? You can't just *kill* this poor old man, who's a guest in our house. If there's even a chance you're wrong here, you need to put on the brakes."

"And if I'm right?"

"If this man is Whitey, I promise you right now he will not leave this house a free man. You think I want Whitey running around out there? Especially if he's doing stuff like this? No, if he has the nerve to show up here like this, he's done for."

"Promise?"

"Promise."

Chapter Eight

Rose barely left her room for a week. She neglected to do her chores. She neglected her canned preserves business, which Joseph carried on for her so that she didn't lose entire days of apple harvest. She refused to visit the site of April's new restaurant, to help set things up before the big opening. She refused to even go for her solo foraging walks in the forest. Most meals she would take in her room. April would bring her a plate or bowl. Sometimes she would eat downstairs, but she barely lifted her face from her plate and ate in silence, then dropped her plate in the sink and retreated upstairs, back to her room, without a word. She seemed emptied out.

Rose also hadn't seen Micah in weeks. The first week had been difficult. She hadn't quite realized just how accustomed she had become to seeing him around, watching him take his dirty work boots off before coming in for dinner, or hearing him talk to Joseph outside, while she worked or rested in the house. She'd gotten more used to the feeling, too, of being watched by him. How it sometimes felt overwhelming but sometimes felt warm and cozy. And also exciting. There wasn't one feeling she'd felt around him, but many. A whole spectrum of feelings. All of that was suddenly gone from her mornings and afternoons and evenings. The anticipation of his arrival, the glow and mellow despair of his departures. All of those feelings were gone.

Well, not quite gone. She still felt them. But they were all in her head now. Memories of feelings, which were fresh enough to feel almost like the live version. But as the first week of his absence gave way to the second week, these feelings started to give way, too. They began to fade. A whole morning would pass during which she would have not a single thought about Micah. Then whole days would pass that way. Inevitably something would come along and remind her, and a feeling of some kind would rush back. But even these feelings were themselves growing thinner and less vivid. By the third week, she felt she was becoming free of him.

Then one morning he was back. Rose heard his voice outside. She was lying in bed and it was his voice and Joseph's that woke her. At first she thought she was dreaming. But then, when it was clear that she was awake, she got out of bed and drifted toward the window. There he was, helping Joseph unload a bunch of plywood that he'd ordered.

Rose watched them unloading the wood for a moment, and then she heard April's voice behind her.

"I'm sorry about that, Rosie," April said, leaning against the door into the hall. "I didn't know he was going to be on this delivery. I would have said something."

"Oh, it's okay," Rose said. "I'm over it."

Rose turned back to the window and quietly continued watching.

A few hours later, after Micah had finished his work and eaten lunch with Joseph and April at the picnic bench under the maple tree, Rose appeared at the door of the house. She had chosen her outfit very carefully: She wore a blue Amish dress, modest according to Amish sensibilities, and also passable as work clothes. Most of her energy had been spent on her meticulously but subtly applied makeup and hair.

Rose walked by, confident and determined, with a foraging basket slung over her shoulder. When Micah noticed her, he turned to watch her. She smiled politely and lifted her hand in greeting. But as she reached them at the picnic table, she didn't slow down. And for a moment they all watched her make her way to the forest alone.

Rose spent much of her time reading. And when she wasn't reading, she was thinking about the mysterious man who'd come to her house, the man she believed was Whitey. She hadn't seen him the next morning. She had heard him talking with April and Joseph. She could smell the pancakes that April had made him. When he left, she watched him from her window. She watched him climb, with great difficulty, into their buggy. And she watched Joseph drive off with him. She didn't get another look at his face.

When the buggy was out of sight, April had immediately appeared at the door to Rose's room.

"Rosie, he's gone."

"I know."

"Joe's taking him to back to his family."

Rose turned away from the window and faced her sister.

"Last night, right after he went off to bed, so shortly before we went to sleep, his brother or cousin or something showed up. He ran into Joseph while he was cleaning up in the barn. He was looking for his relative. Because it turns out this guy disappears from his family without warning, sometimes for a long time, like weeks, and just lives in the woods. He's got all kinds of problems, and Joseph said that the relative was also kind of weird himself. Anyway, they get worried and start looking for him in the area. But he and Joseph agreed that he should stay put for the night, since the guy was already asleep, and they agreed that Joseph would take him back home this morning. So . . . you see? This guy is who he said he was."

Rose didn't reply. She knew she would never convince her sister, or anyone, about what she knew to be true. She knew that this story could easily have been concocted, that some cousin character could easily be recruited to help sell the story. But she didn't say anything because she knew that such talk would make her sound crazy. But she was not crazy. Not at all. Whitey was crazy; she was not.

"So that's it?" Rose said.

"That's it, Rosie. Let's try to put this behind us. It was a bad night for all of us. But I want you to know that we're keeping you safe here. Joseph, by the way, stayed up all night and had his gun in our room, ready to go, just in case."

"Joseph has a gun?"

"Apparently. I didn't even know he did. I kind of laughed when he said it because he's so not a gun guy. And he's not supposed to have one. The community doesn't encourage it. But, after everything that happened, he decided we needed to have an emergency security back-up plan. So apparently he's got a gun stashed away."

"That's good to know, I guess."

"He just wants us all to be safe."

"So Joseph wasn't totally convinced by this guy's story, either?"

"He was just taking precautions, Rosie."

Later that day a horse and buggy appeared at the end of the long drive connecting the farm to the road. It could only have been coming their way. Rose looked at April, but she just shrugged. For a moment, they paused at the window to watch it approach. Without a word, April disappeared, and Rose heard her footsteps on the stairs and then heard the sound of April locking the front and back doors. Then she came back up to Rose, just as the buggy was nearing the house. It wasn't unusual to get an unannounced visit from a neighbor or from one of Joseph's family. Even so, this was a horse and a buggy that they didn't recognize. And, after the appearance of the old man, April was taking no chances.

"Ugh, what is this about?" April said under her breath as the buggy came to a stop behind the barn, and a man jumped out and tied his horse there. They couldn't make out who it was, only that it was one person, alone. As soon as he started walking toward the house, Rose knew who it was. She knew that gait. And when he passed in front of the barn, a bag slung over his shoulder, they could see his face, and her hunch was confirmed. Micah.

April rolled her eyes at Rose.

"This was not planned," April said. "He shouldn't be here."

"It's fine, Ri," Rose replied. "I'm not going to dissolve into a heap of tears."

The knock came.

"Go answer it," Rose said. "It's *fine*."

Rose, suddenly overcome by exhaustion, lay down on her bed. She could just barely hear April downstairs, unlatching the door and chatting with Micah. April giggled more than usual. Was *she* flirting with him now? *He's addicted to charming the ladies,* she thought. Even though she couldn't make out what they were saying, she did like hearing his voice. The tenor of it, the way she could hear the smile in it. *Ugh, Mr. Charmer.*

A minute later April came back upstairs. Rose didn't move from her position, lying on her side on the made bed. When she turned her eyes up, she saw April standing in the doorway, her face glowing with a big grin.

"Ri," Rose said, half into her pillow, "get a hold of yourself. You're a married woman."

April laughed merrily.

"What?" she said.

"Forget it," Rose said. "But seriously, why are you grinning like that? And . . . what are you hiding back there?"

April pulled her hand out from behind her back and presented a tiny black mewing fur ball of a kitten.

"Ta-da!"

"Omi*god!*" Rose said, quickly pulling herself up from the bed. "It's so squeaky!"

"Do you want to hold him?"

April placed the tiny cat on Rose's shoulder, and his little paws spread and he immediately latched onto Rose's T-shirt. She petted his head and he relaxed a bit and squeaked back appreciatively.

"Oh, Ri, he's perfect."

"I know! He's such a good boy. You can already tell."

"*This* is why Micah dropped by?"

"Yup. He found this little guy at his sister's house. And they had no idea where it came from. They looked everywhere for the mom or siblings. Nothing."

"Oh," Rose said. "That's really sad." April looked as if she regretted giving her the whole backstory.

"But this is a happy ending!"

"Yeah, I guess."

"He brought it . . . for you, actually," April added.

"What makes you say that?"

"Because he told me! He said, 'Does Rose want a kitten?' And then he said, 'When I met this guy, I thought about her right away.' That's exactly what he said. And I was like, 'Look, we'll give the kitten a good home here' because, you know, I don't want this Micah guy bothering you with his charming kittens."

"Yeah, exactly," Rose said. "And what does he mean 'I thought about her right away'? What would that little fiancée of his think of *that?*"

"Right?" April said.

Rose set the kitten down on the floor. And he began

pouncing on her foot, as though hunting it. And then he'd get upset when his tiny claws got stuck in her sock.

"But anyway," she said, "it *was* kind of nice of him to think of me."

"I'm guessing he thinks about you a lot."

Later that night, as they were cleaning up, Rose suddenly said, "What is his deal, though?" She was sweeping up the floor, then emptying the dustpan into the garbage.

"You mean . . , Micah?" April asked from the sink where she was washing dishes.

"Um, *yeah,* obviously Micah," Rose said, making a beeline for the sofa, where she immediately plopped down and rolled herself in a blanket. "What's his deal? Why is he so . . . Mr. Entertainer-Guy?"

"He means well."

"When I was around him my face literally hurt from smiling constantly at his banter."

"He can be a bit much."

"*Ri,* he's a bit more than a bit much."

"He's been through a lot."

"Oh, really? Because I was kidnapped by a literal psycho. But do I stare at you with these massive eyes to make sure you're laughing at my jokes?"

Rose stared at April with exaggeratedly unblinking eyes. April laughed.

"Okay, he does do that," she said. "But he does have nice eyes, doesn't he?"

"When they're not beaming down on me . . . I guess?"

"Well, you don't have to hang out with him if you don't want. I can tell Joseph to keep him away."

"Ugh, I dunno . . ." said Rose, and trailed off. "Well," Rose added after a moment, "what *is* his deal? You said he's been through a lot. What has he been through?"

"Oh, Rose, do you really want to know?"

"Now you *have* to tell me."

"One day he was driving his buggy—"

"Okay, you're right," Rose cut in. "I don't want to hear this."

"I didn't think so."

"Tell me anyway!"

April stared at Rose for a long second.

"Tell me!"

"Seriously?"

"Yes, seriously! I want to know."

So she told her. Micah was driving his buggy to town one evening. It was starting to get dark. His sister was in the buggy with him. They were struck by a speeding Ford F-150 that had come zipping around a blind corner. The buggy was totaled. Micah emerged with scratches and a broken arm. His sister, who was sitting in the back, was killed. But she hadn't died right away. Micah sat with her by the side of the road for half an hour before an ambulance came. It happened a bit more than two years ago. She left two children, a one-year-old and three-year-old, Micah's nieces.

Rose got quiet and distant. It was obvious that April regretted telling Rose this story. Then Rose had questions.

"Did she die on the road or in the hospital?"

"What kind of question is that? I don't know."

"What did she say—what were her last words?"

"Rose, I don't know."

"What about the driver of the truck?"

"What about him?"

"I dunno. What do we know about him?"

"Not much. It was a hit-and-run. They eventually caught him. He claimed he didn't realize what happened. Thought he hit a deer and wasn't going to stop for that."

"He was lying, right?"

"Probably. He wasn't drunk or anything. But they did charge him."

"And Micah?"

"Poor Micah. You can imagine how torn up he is over it. He blames himself, even though there's literally nothing he could have done. He was very close to this sister. And is super close to her kids."

Rose got quiet. April continued.

"Joseph said he changed a lot after the accident."

"How?"

"Not sure."

"Seriously, Ri? How do you not ask these things?"

"I'm not as nosy as you."

Rose rolled her eyes.

"Anyway," April said. "Should I tell Joseph to keep Micah away so you don't have to laugh at his jokes?"

Rose thought for a moment.

"Nah, it's okay," Rose said quietly. "You don't need to tell Joseph anything."

Chapter Nine

That week Rose threw a small birthday party for April. And it was small because everyone was too busy to party. April was working to launch her restaurant, the thing she'd been dreaming about for years. She had carefully developed each dish on her seasonal menu, crafted to match what was best and freshest in the region. She had even gotten better and more committed to foraging in the forest near her house so that the mushrooms and herbs on her menu were the finest available. Her restaurant would appeal to people in Lancaster who wanted locally grown fine food in a low-key, unpretentious environment. In keeping with Amish norms, it would be a breakfast and lunch place (supper was a time to be home with the family), and it would be closed on Sunday. It would also appeal to tourists who'd come to Amish country looking for good local food with a nod to Amish tradition.

Planning the menus was work, of course, but it was the fun part of the job. The hard and not fun part was staying on top of the financing, raising the capital to launch a risky enterprise. Convincing Carmen, her mentor in both life and food, to be an investor had not been easy. Carmen believed in April fully. But launching a restaurant was about as risky a venture as could be. And Carmen's own risky venture, a bakery in downtown Philly, was finally in the black for the first time. She had very little room to absorb any major losses. Even so, it was a risk she was willing to take. She looked at her books, prepared for the potential loss, and found ways to offset it. Her biggest fear was April herself. Or, more to the point, her relationship with April. Carmen had been around long enough to see how business partnerships could tear apart relationships. And not just if the businesses failed. Successful ventures posed their own kind of threat to relationships. Tensions almost felt like a certainty, a no-win situation for their relationship.

"We've been through so much together," Carmen said to April one day as they chatted over the phone. "I can't imagine losing you."

April was silent for a moment. She sighed and said, "I'm listening to what you're saying."

She wanted Carmen to think that she was listening deeply to what she was saying, that she was weighing her words, her wisdom, as carefully as possible. But it simply wasn't true. April was young and brash. She was absolutely certain that this business would succeed and that her relationship with Carmen wouldn't be affected, except possibly that the joint venture would bring them even closer together. April had no hesitations, but she was clever and she knew that her mentor and friend would not be persuaded by her certainty. So she feigned hesitation.

And she wasn't completely faking it, either. She was, in fact, carefully choosing her words, trying to put them together just right so that Carmen would stop being so annoying and just get on board already. Finally she spoke.

"Well," she said, "I think you said it best yourself: *We've been through so much together*. That's just it! We've been through harder things than this. We can do this, too."

But Carmen was still not convinced. Until, one day, when she'd made the drive to central Pennsylvania to visit, and saw how Rose felt about the new business. They had all made the trip to Lancaster to show Carmen one of the potential sites for their future restaurant. When the property manager had turned the key to open up the space, Rose almost ran in. She excitedly pulled up the blinds, letting in a glorious wave of sunlight.

"Here it is!" she said, taking a bow. "We could set up some tables outside, too."

Then she ran over to another wall and said, "We could turn this wall into a big picture window so you can look into the kitchen and stuff. We asked the owner and he was cool with it. Right?" she said, turning to the property manager who'd let them in. He nodded and smiled at Rose's enthusiasm.

Rose then darted to the other side of the space to talk about the long wood tables that Micah and Joseph could make by hand. On and on she went about how *perfect* the custom-fitted tables were going to be in this space. And as she spoke, Carmen turned to April, who gave her a knowing look. Afterward, April wandered over to Carmen.

"Rose is pretty excited about this," April said.

Carmen gave April a skeptical look.

"C'mon, you can't deny it," April said.

"Oh, I'm not denying it," Carmen replied. "I'm just. . . . You didn't put her up to this, right?"

"What! Of course not," April said.

"I'm only joking. Well, half joking."

"No, she's really excited about the restaurant. And you know that's a big deal, Carmen. You know hard it is to get her out of her shell these days."

"I do," Carmen said.

Chapter Ten

They were running late for a Saturday picnic hosted by one of Joseph's cousins. Rose hadn't decided whether she was going or not. Even as April and Joseph got ready, Rose sat on her bed, uncertain.

"Rosie? Coming or not?" April called from across the hall.

"I dunno," Rose replied. But she was already getting herself dressed.

At the picnic, Rose found herself a spot on a bench and she decided, then and there, to commit herself to this spot for the duration of the afternoon. She was already regretting her decision to go to this event. How had she forgotten that she hated picnics? If she wanted to eat her lunch sitting in an uncomfortable position while brushing ants out of her hair and getting bitten by a mosquito on the back of her neck at the precise moment she tried to bite into her potato salad, she could at least do these things at home, with the peace of solitude. But here she had the additional burden of making small talk.

They were very friendly folks. The worst kind. Rose

loved them deeply, for all the support they were giving
her. But chitchat was, to her, a soul-exploding exercise.
And what was the point of it all? She would make conversation so forgettable that she herself could barely remember what she'd said a second earlier. Worse, she
would have to make herself seem agreeable, which meant
avoiding any topic that might seem too real, too close to
where her mind actually lived these days. She would have
to censor herself, filter her negativity, edit out her sar-
casm. The whole thing just seemed exhausting.

"Hey, champ," someone said.

It was a man, of course. He plopped his large body
down next to her, almost catapulting her off the rickety
bench at first—and indeed sending the coleslaw that she
was trying to eat flying off her fork—and then sending
her in the other direction, hurtling at him, until she was
pinned against his arm.

"Oops, sorry about that!" he said, backing up quickly
to give her space.

"It's fine," she muttered as she scooted back to the spot
she'd committed herself to for the afternoon. After she
was settled again, she identified this interloper. It was
Micah. Of course it was.

"Didn't mean to launch your coleslaw there," he said.
His dimples winked at her.

"Yeah, I was kind of enjoying that coleslaw."

"I'm sorry," he said. *Dimples*.

"You don't seem sorry," she said, trying to suppress a
smile.

"I'm very sorry," he said, putting his hand over his

heart and bowing his neck gallantly. Then he looked at her again. Those dimples weren't getting less distracting.

"Wait, did you call me *'champ'?*" she said.

"I did!"

"You're seriously a very corny individual," she said.

"Do you find kittens corny?"

"Micah," Rose said, looking at him with uncharacteristic directness. "Kittens are literally the corniest thing on earth. They're almost as bad as rainbows and sunsets and red, red roses."

"Okay, true. But it's different when it's *your* kitten, isn't it? And how is that kitty doing? What are you naming him?"

"Snowflake," she said, unable to keep from smiling.

"Snowflake! And that's not corny?"

"Actually, no, it's not corny. Not in this case," she said.

"Why is that?"

"Because it's *clever,* Micah. Snowflake the cat, as you know, is all black. Nothing snowy white about him."

"I was going to ask about that."

"Well, then, ask!"

"Why did you name a black cat Snowflake?"

"Ugh," Rose said, returning to her coleslaw. "If you have to ask, you wouldn't understand anyway."

Micah looked as if he couldn't tell whether Rose was joking now, or whether she was actually annoyed with him.

"I'm sorry for being kind of dumb about some things," Micah said. "But I really do want to know."

"Awright," Rose said, putting her fork down. "I'm not going to spell this out completely for you. Because . . . I dunno why. I guess I don't totally trust you"—Micah winced a bit, Rose noticed—"Sorry. Just being real with you. But how about this. I'll give you, like, a clue. Snowflake is . . . a state of mind."

"A state of mind," Micah repeated. "Okay. I'll think about that."

"Don't think too hard, champ," Rose said. "What would your future *wife* say?"

And then, suddenly inspired to take a walk, Rose jumped up, knocked the brim of Micah's cap down over his face, and began walking off before he could lift it back into place. Rose desperately wanted to look back at him, partly to see the expression on his face, and partly just to see that face once more. She was also dying to see if he was looking around, if he was nervous whether his fiancée, or someone else, was watching. But she resisted the temptation and continued walking.

Chapter Eleven

Rose had not been to April's restaurant in weeks. When she walked in, she almost gasped. The place was completely transformed. The floors were redone, now a mix of hardwood, and in and around the kitchen, a checkerboard tile. The bleak office-building drop ceiling had been removed, revealing an ornate mid-century tin ceiling behind it. It had been in such bad condition when they poked through that nobody could even see the beautiful original ceiling. But April had done her homework. She'd consulted architecture historians and even managed to find, in the local library, some photos of the space as it had looked originally, including some tantalizing flashes of that ceiling. She knew it was there and had directed her workmen to scratch and scrub until they found it. And they did. Rose had been there when they had finally worked their way through the layers to reveal a swatch of that ceiling. But now the drop ceiling was gone and the entire original ceiling was revealed, and it was truly glorious.

Joseph and some of his rotating crew were now busy outfitting the place with new woodwork—some shelving and some beautiful ornamental flourishes like a banister that ran along the half wall separating the restaurant's two main seating areas, and some wood paneling on the walls. Once they were done with that, they would fabricate the restaurant's tables and chairs.

"It's gonna be insanely cool," April said to Rose as they walked around. "Like magazine-level awesome."

"I'm in total shock," Rose said, as she ran her hand over the unfinished banister. "It's exactly how I was picturing it."

April beamed.

"Oh, come here," she said, grabbing Rose's hand and pulling her away. "I wanna show you something."

She pulled her into the kitchen.

"Don't look at the kitchen yet," she said, "it's a total mess in here. They've barely even started. But I made sure they put this in first. . . ." April jumped to the side. "Ta-da!"

On the wall, where she had been standing, were three hooks, mounted on a polished wooden board. Over one, the name APRIL was etched into the wood, over the next, JOSEPH, and over the third hook the name ROSE was etched.

"This is where we'll keep our aprons," April said.

"That's unbelievably cheesy."

"I know, right? I couldn't help myself!"

"I mean, I do love it, though," Rose said, running her fingers over her etched name. "The carving is really beautiful."

"It looks pretty good, don't you think?" The voice came from behind them. Rose turned around and saw Micah standing there, holding a sledgehammer.

"It's okay," Rose said.

"Made it myself," Micah said, setting the top of the hammer on the ground, and leaning on the handle.

"Nice hammer," Rose said. "I don't think it's ginormous enough, though."

"He's trying to look tough," April said.

"It's not working," Rose said.

The dimples came, and they were accompanied by something new.

"No! Are you literally blushing now?" Rose said, walking toward him and studying his face as she walked. Micah seemed determined to say something but was unable to form a word.

"We shouldn't make too much fun of Micah," April said. "The truth is he's doing a great job in here. And he did really carve those names on there. That was all him."

Rose turned to look at the names again. The work was meticulous. Joseph suddenly popped his head into the kitchen.

"April," he said, "can you come here for a second? I wanna show you something."

April shot a glance at Rose.

"Go ahead," Rose said to April. "I'm fine."

Now that Rose and Micah were alone in the kitchen, a palpable awkwardness settled between them.

"She's always watching out for you," Micah said.

"She's my sister," Rose replied, slightly more curtly than she had intended.

"I didn't mean it in a bad way . . . just . . ."

"I know," Rose said. "I wasn't trying to be sarcastic. Just, yeah, she watches over me because she's my sister. She's protective, too, because I've been through a lot."

"Oh," Micah said.

She could tell he wanted to ask. A part of her wanted him to ask. A part of her would have bitten his head off if he had. She was relieved and grateful that he didn't.

"I've been through some things, too," Micah said. "So I understand, sort of."

Rose suddenly remembered Micah's story. She winced now, thinking about what she'd said. Given what had happened to his own sister, maybe talking about the importance of sisters was not the right thing to bring up. She'd noticed a change in his face when she had. A vulnerability in the eyes, a slight pursing of the mouth, a slight downcast change in the angle of his gaze that told Rose Micah was also thinking about his sister. She looked at this man and he seemed suddenly small and vulnerable and childlike. She couldn't even begin to imagine what it would be like to lose her own sister, and especially the way he'd lost his. She had to fight the urge to throw her arms around him and apologize and tell him that everything was going to be okay. She had to fight the urge, in fact, to say anything that indicated she knew of his loss. She wanted so badly to let him know that she understood, but in trying to figure out how to signal any of this, she instead said nothing at all, and just stared.

"I should get back," he said, gesturing toward the dining area.

"Back to pretending to use your big, manly hammer?" she said, and immediately regretted her words.

"Yeah," he said, and, giving Rose the world's smallest and briefest and saddest smile, he turned around and disappeared through the kitchen's swinging doors.

Chapter Twelve

Rose went back to the restaurant with April every day that week. Supposedly she was going there to help April set up. But she had other thoughts, too.

"Is Micah going to be around today?" she asked April on the buggy ride over. The day before, Micah had been absent. And his absence had been somewhat mysterious. They had expected him to be there with the rest of the work crew.

"Yeah, he should be there," April said absently as she looked out at the fields passing by. "Though he wasn't there yesterday for some reason."

"I know," Rose said.

April looked at Rose.

"I said something dumb to him the other day," Rose said. "And I kind of wanted to apologize or whatever."

"How bad could it have been?" April said, returning her gaze to the fields.

"He seemed pretty upset," Rose said. "Or not upset, but like, sad."

"Well, he's got some drama going on in his life."

"Yeah, that was kind of the problem. I forgot about

what he's been going through and put my foot in my mouth."

Now April turned quickly to her sister.

"Wait," she said. "Are we talking about the same thing?"

"Well . . . what are *you* talking about?"

"No, you first!"

"I'm talking about what you told me. About the accident. About losing his sister . . ."

"Oh, no, no," April said, "I'm not talking about that. I mean, yeah, that's always part of his sadness. But no, I'm talking about a different drama."

"Okay, out with it!"

"He recently broke up with his fiancée," April said.

"Oh, that *is* drama."

"At least, I think they broke up. They definitely decided to break off the engagement. They're not getting married. That much I know."

"How did you not tell me this?" Rose said, just as the buggy pulled up to the back of the restaurant.

"I don't know, Rose," April said. "When it comes to Micah, I sometimes lose track of what you want to know and what you don't."

"Well, *now* I want to know everything!"

"Okay," April said, as she opened the buggy door and stepped out. "Good to know."

The moment the door of the restaurant opened, she saw him. She walked past Micah with a small smile. "Just here to work," she murmured to him as she walked by.

"Okay, then," he replied.

They sat quietly for a few long minutes as Micah worked at his bench, measuring out some wooden planks, cutting each one carefully with a small handsaw, and then stacking them by the door to the kitchen. Rose sat at the one of the restaurant's oak tables, which Micah had just recently made. She scanned her phone and a large pile of old cookbooks—which she'd picked up in thrift shops—searching for alluring recipes, or even just interesting combinations of ingredients, and she dog-eared the pages and scribbled in one of her notebooks. She had a notebook for summer, fall, winter, and spring. April had taught her all about seasonal cooking and taught her, too, how to research recipe ideas. Occasionally Rose would peer out over her sprawling stacks of books and notebooks and catch a glimpse of Micah squatting down to measure something, or bearing down on a plank. She watched his strong shoulder holding the plank in place, and the other arm worked it over with the saw.

But mostly she worked. April had given her the task of scouting out winter dishes. She was to track down as many ways as possible to prepare root vegetables. She found the work absorbing. She would sink deep into the recipes and the stories around the recipes, and before she knew it, hours would go by.

"I'm not getting married," Micah suddenly blurted out from his workstation.

"What?" Rose shouted back across the room, pointing to her ear. She could barely hear him over the sound of the hammering in the next room.

"*I'm not getting married,*" he shouted back. He got up and walked to her, then leaned against the table where she was working.

"Oh," she said to him. "I'm sorry about that."

"It's for the best," he said.

"I've broken up like a million times," she said.

She felt suddenly self-conscious because of the look he was giving her.

"But it was always for the best," she said.

"Would you like to come to my niece's birthday party?" he blurted out again. "Sorry to change the subject."

"Were you changing the subject?" she said, unable to conceal a sly smile.

"I, uh . . ."

Rose gave Micah a long look. He seemed confident at all times, but when she watched him carefully, she realized he was more awkward than he let on. He had a habit of rising onto his tiptoes and rocking just a slight bit when he was nervous. It was a very reliable, and a very winning tell, she thought.

"I, uh . . ." he said, climbing up on his tiptoes.

"I would love to go to your niece's birthday party," Rose said.

The birthday party was far more elaborate than Rose was expecting. Without anyone telling her, she was sure that all the details had been planned and executed by Micah himself. He had, it seemed, bought out an entire party store of every possible kiddie birthday item. An armada of balloons, Baby Shark-themed tablecloths, plates, and cups. Toy centerpieces made of pinwheels and bigger pinwheels and even bigger pinwheels. The cake, purchased from Kroger per the birthday girl's instructions, was massive, and the ice cream selection almost as extensive as an ice cream shop's. Micah's family seemed put off by the excess, which was decidedly un-Amish. But Micah's niece was in heaven.

Rose was amused at the bumblingly male way that Micah had put together this celebration. He'd bought too much stuff and nothing quite made sense. Nothing was presented correctly. Everything was a bit off-kilter. But all of it moved Rose deeply, to see how much effort he'd put into it all to make his little orphaned niece's birthday something special.

And the highlight of the day was the gift he gave his niece: a brand-new tree house that he'd secretly made for her in a large maple on the edge of the family's cornfield. When Rose saw this tree house, her jaw dropped.

"Micah, it's *gorgeous*," she whispered to him as they walked toward it. "That's a *house*. I would live in that happily."

He opened his mouth to say something. Then decided not to say a thing. But Rose saw his intention. And Micah saw her see it. And they both laughed.

Chapter Thirteen

One night, shortly after dinner, the police paid a visit. There were two of them: Officers Dunford and Bielby. Not local cops, but Pennsylvania State Police, Joseph noticed when he answered the door.

"This isn't the easiest place to find," Bielby said without saying hello.

"You guys seem to have a lot of trouble finding people," Rose observed quietly from the couch.

She could hear April chuckling from the kitchen, where she was doing dishes.

"Have you seen anything suspicious around here?" Bielby asked.

Rose was now standing behind Joseph at the door.

"Do you know who I am?" she asked them.

"Should we?"

She told them about Whitey, about the kidnapping.

"Yeah, we've heard about that," Dunford said. "Is there anything you want to report about it now?"

"I'm sometimes afraid that he's . . . around," Rose said to them. "That he's close. Watching."

"Unlikely," Bielby said. "Even though we've always suspected he has a base nearby. . . ."

"He does," Rose said. "I know that for a fact. And I've reported it."

". . . but anyway, he's on the run now. So I doubt he's near. Probably in Mexico or in the desert. To be honest, he's got other things on his mind than snooping around here. I wouldn't worry too much about it. Feds are on it."

April, who'd also drifted toward the door, looked upset when the police told her not to worry about it.

"Well, we have good reason to be concerned," April said. "Wait here for a second."

She ran upstairs and came down with a crumpled piece of paper in her hand.

"I found this," April said. "A note. Left here."

She looked at Rose. "I wasn't going to tell you. But . . . now I think I should."

She held up the note. It read *I am always watching you.*

"Why didn't you tell me?" Rose said.

"Rosie, you know why. You're only just starting to feel comfortable here. But it's time to be honest. Your fears are not just in your head. I want you to feel safe here, but I also don't want to lie to you. I want you to feel okay, but I also don't want you to feel like you're going insane with paranoid thoughts. You're not going insane. You're not paranoid. That stranger wasn't Whitey that night. I'm still sure of that. But you *aren't* imagining that he's around. He is. I want you to know that, so you can trust your senses again. And I want you also to know: we *will* keep you safe here. If it becomes unsafe, we will leave. We have a plan for that, too. You will be fine. Right now, though, it's just as important to know that, *no,* you're not losing your mind, and, *yes*, we do believe you, okay?"

"Okay," Rose said. "Thank you, Ri. I'm glad you're telling me the truth. Sometimes I feel like you shield me too much."

"I know I do," April said.

"And you don't need to. You know I'm Philly tough. Remember Grady?"

"Of course," April said.

"Remember when I kicked his ass all over South Street and Seventh, on both sides of the street? Smashed his dumb face into a mailbox. Threatened to throw him into the street if he didn't agree to shut his mouth."

Rose looked over at the cops for a moment.

"We were just kids," Rose said to them. "This was a long time ago."

"Believe me, I remember," April said. "You're my tough little sister."

April went over to Rose and gave her a big hug. Tears unexpectedly filled April's eyes.

The cops were starting to get antsy.

"I know this is hard," Bielby said. "These things are never easy."

"Can we get back to the questions, though?" Dunford added. "That note . . ."

"Here it is," April said, as she walked over to the cop and handed it to him.

"Where did you find the note?"

"In the couch," April said, "under that cushion. I was cleaning there one day and lifted the cushion, and it was right there, the message facing me."

"And when did you find the note?"

"Last week," April said.

"Why didn't you report it?" the other cop cut in.

"I did," April said. "I called in."

"Really?"

"Yeah, *really,*" April said. "Why do I always feel like I'm getting accused of something when I talk to you people?"

"We're sorry about that," Bielby said. "We're just trying to get a clear picture."

"Why are you even here right now?" April said.

"We got a call," Dunford said. "About a disturbance here. Caller claimed they lived in this house."

"None of us called you about that," April said.

Chapter Fourteen

That night, Rose woke up shortly before 3:00 A.M.. Again. She was instantly wide awake. And alert. She got out of bed and went to the window. She didn't know what was compelling her to do this, but she knew without a doubt that there was something she needed to see through the window immediately, something that was waiting out there for her to see, something she had been waiting to see for a while. She felt a sense of tardiness. As if she was late for something important.

She threw open the curtain. Her room filled with moonlight. The moon was full and the sky was mostly clear. Outside, on the lawn in front of the barn, a young woman stood. She was looking up. She was looking directly at Rose.

Rose quickly dropped down out of sight. Her heart was pounding, her breath short. Her palms were sweaty. It was a ghost. Rose knew it was. Yet it was real. Even as her body cycled through every fear response, she recognized that at heart she was not scared. She took a moment to breathe, and to think. If she wasn't scared, what *was* this feeling? The feeling that she was too late came back. And with it, a feeling of shame.

But she wasn't afraid of this girl outside, she realized. No, she was interested in seeing her. Talking to her. Going to her. She . . . knew this girl.

Rose lifted her head toward the window again for another peek. And when her eyes reached the window, she was face-to-face with the girl. The girl was on the roof, crouching right in front of her window. Staring in. Staring into her window with large, unblinking eyes. This time, Rose felt real fear. She was so startled, she fell backward and threw her hand over her mouth so that she didn't scream.

Now, in a seated position on her floor, looking up at the window, her hand over her mouth, her eyes wide in fright and wonder and disbelief, she saw that the girl was mimicking her pose exactly: her hand was over her mouth, her eyes wide. And she stayed in this pose, like a statue, even as Rose got herself up on her feet. She went over to the window.

Rose opened the window. Slowly, so as not to make too much noise. The girl did not move. Rose could see her big, tired brown eyes, her skin glowing in the moonlight, her black hair streaming down over her shoulders. Rose opened her mouth, unsure what she wanted to say. And, almost involuntarily, the name of the girl came right out of her mouth.

And then Rose woke up. For real this time. She was lying in bed, on her side. Her sheet was gone, rolled onto the floor. She was drenched in sweat. She looked over at her window. The curtain was wide open, which was odd, since she was nearly certain she'd closed it. Moonlight poured in. That was what had woken her.

Or maybe it was her own voice that woke her. She'd heard the voice just as she came out of the dream. It was her voice, wasn't it? It was her voice, saying the girl's name. But now she was awake. And she didn't need to go to the window to know that the girl was not there. Instead, she closed her eyes and tried to re-enter the dream gently. She wanted so badly to see the girl again, to speak to her. She tried to relax her body and her mind, to let herself drift off. And it worked. She drifted. But just for a moment. It was not enough. She was awake. Her conscious mind was working too hard. The dream was fading fast.

She needed to know the girl's name. She knew the name. She'd said the name. It had been on her lips only seconds earlier. She'd said it aloud. She'd heard it. What was it? It wasn't Kate, no. And it wasn't Kayleigh. But it was something like that. K . . . something.

Rose knew her. This wasn't a figment of her imagination. It was someone she knew, someone specific. But who? She tried hard to keep the scene in her head. She wanted to write it down but was beginning to feel heavy again with sleep. The way the girl had looked directly at her. The way she was illuminated by the moonlight. The way she mimicked Rose's gestures. The way she appeared on the roof, looked directly into her window. The strange light. The feelings surrounding all this. Not fear. No, this was not a scary dream, but it was uncanny. It felt more like a vision than a dream. And that strange emotion, of arriving late, also came back clearly to Rose, an emotion as clear in her mind as something she could see, as three-dimensional as the girl herself. *Carly*.

* * *

In Whitey's closed compound, Rose had cycled through a range of emotions: sometimes the blinders were off and she saw things with utter clarity. And in those moments, she hated Whitey and wanted nothing more than to escape. Other times she was lulled by him into contentment. She accepted the idea that this place was where her real life was happening, and that the outside world, the world she had come from, was the fake reality. There were moments when submitting to this vision gave Rose a feeling of peace and of purpose. She could be mesmerized by his stories and by the setting. And by the other women who were there, Whitey's acolytes.

Later, once she was free, she would come to realize that these women were a very deliberate part of Whitey's scheme. If they were able to persuade newcomers to stay in the Community, they would remain. When Rose felt contentment at the compound, those moments when she felt that maybe this place was where she belonged, it was the women, not Whitey, who made that seem possible. And when the illusion felt weak, and Rose felt trapped, she wasn't sure what to think, or say, or how to act around the other women.

The exception was Carly. Carly didn't seem brainwashed. She was the only one like that. She went along with everything that was happening in the compound. But at no point did she ever affect the faraway demeanor, the dreamy way of speaking, the lingo-heavy language of Whitey's cultists. She seemed self-possessed. And though she never spoke out against Whitey nor, from what Rose had observed, actively defied him, she did make small gestures of resistance. A sigh during one of his lectures. A bored air during his endless meditation sessions. Once in a while, Rose swore she'd seen her roll her eyes at Whitey. And once she caught her smirking at something he'd said.

Once, their eyes had met. Carly was smirking slyly. And when she saw that Rose was watching her, she had suppressed the smirk. But it didn't work. In fact, it had the opposite effect. The smirk grew into a full giggle. Carly immediately put her hand over her mouth to gain some control but, seeing Rose and seeing that Rose herself was beginning to smile, Carly had a full-on giggle attack. When the others started noticing, and when Whitey noticed, Carly had buried her face in her hands, and pretended to be sobbing—wailing—to cover for her laughter. And when another one of the women had gone over to Carly to comfort her, she had brushed her away, saying, "I'm okay, just overwhelmed by beauty." Then she once again caught Rose's eye, saw Rose's own barely suppressed grin, and fell into yet another giggle fit (and yet more "wailing").

Later that night, Carly had drifted by Rose's cell. Like all the women in the compound, Rose was reluctant to speak openly about her feelings, especially any negative feelings or any doubts she might have had about Whitey and his "community." Even if she felt she could trust someone, there was always the fear that Whitey himself was listening, or watching, or both. Every space was wired. There were microphones and cameras everywhere.

But, even if there weren't, the trust question ran deep: Who in this compound could you trust? There were generally three kinds of people there. Those who worked for

Whitey. Those who'd been brainwashed by him. And those who'd been kidnapped by him and lived in fear of him. Rose herself was struggling against the brainwashing efforts of Whitey. Half the time she barely trusted herself. She certainly didn't want to take the risk of sharing her doubts and feelings with one of Whitey's followers.

But Carly seemed different. Even before the giggling fit, there had been signs that Carly was not brainwashed by Whitey. And that she, in fact, did not want to be here at all. She kept her feelings to herself. She hid them, in fact, as best she could. And most people seemed not to notice. Probably Whitey himself did notice. And Rose noticed. And the giggle fit confirmed her suspicion. It brought them into a secret understanding. Not quite an alliance. Not yet, at least. But something had happened there. Something had been communicated. Carly had seen Rose notice, and she was just fine with that. And later that day Carly was standing in her doorway.

"I've always been like that," Carly was saying to Rose.

"Like what?" Rose said, as she organized her small bedstand.

"I.L.: Inappropriate Laughter," Carly said. "I'd get I.L. in school *a lot*. Sometimes at home, when my mom was trying to be serious about something. But the worst was in church. For like *years* of my life, my mom was basically afraid to take me to church."

They both laughed.

"They would come home from the church meeting, all dressed up, and I would be on the couch in my pajamas. And when they walked in, and I saw them, I would just burst out laughing. And my mom would get mad all over again. But, like, it only made her less willing to bring me the next week."

Again they laughed

It felt strange to laugh here, in this place. It *sounded* strange, muffled within the thick walls of the compound. Rose had always been a fun-loving person who'd spent hours laughing with friends. Until Carly had shown up, she hadn't quite realized how little she'd laughed since she'd come into Whitey's world. And how much she missed it. Without even entirely realizing it, some part of her was withering away and dying. But now, with Carly standing in her doorway, a mischievous little smile on her face, Rose was realizing that this part of her wasn't dead. Not at all. She sat down on her cot and looked directly at Carly.

"Sometimes I get confused here," Rose said.

"I do, too. I think . . . we all do, you know?"

A part of Rose was scared by this conversation—if her heart, which was beating almost painfully fast and hard, was any indication, she was even more scared than she'd realized. And yet she was also certain, without a doubt, that Carly was a friend. That this conversation was just between them. Even so, she tiptoed carefully.

"Are you, like, *okay* though?" Rose blurted out.

Carly didn't answer right away. She looked down at her feet for a moment. Then she looked up again, at Rose. Her smile was gone. It was replaced with . . . something else. Something Rose couldn't quite place.

"Yeah," Carly said, nodding and furrowing her brow. "You know what? I am okay. This isn't exactly what I expected. But that's the way a lot of my life has been. I'm Amish. Or I *was*. Did you know that?"

Rose shook her head.

"Yeah. I guess I don't talk about it that much. I think I'm the only one here with that background. Well, besides Whitey himself. I don't talk much to my family. I don't even know if they know I'm gone. They've considered me a lost cause for a while now. That's how I found my way here. One of my cousins worked for Whitey. He also left the community. He kind of introduced me to this place. I didn't expect it to be quite like . . . *this,* you know? But I'm here now. I have what I need to get by. It's better than what I had out there. I was kind of lost. And even though it's kind of intense in here, I feel, I don't know . . ."

"Watched over?" Rose said.

A smile came and left quickly on Carly's face.

"Yeah," Carly said. "Something like that."

Chapter Fifteen

Joseph was uncharacteristically late for dinner. Usually he helped April and Rose cook the food and set the table. But on this night he was nowhere to be found.

"Did he tell you anything?" April said to Rose, as she set out the dinner plates and utensils. Rose was in the kitchen, stirring the rice.

"Did he tell *me* anything?" she said. "Why would he tell me and not you?"

"I dunno," April said. She stopped setting the plates and stared blankly at the table for a moment. "Just trying to figure out what's happening here. This is so unlike him."

April looked at Rose. Because she was behind Rose, she couldn't see her face. But somehow April got the sense, from her body language, that Rose was growing anxious.

"I'm sure it's nothing," April said. "If he's not back in the next ten, we'll just start. He'll join us when he's back."

The minute they sat down to eat, Joseph burst in.

"Micah's gone," he said, breathlessly.

"*What!*" Rose said.

"He's gone," Joseph said.

"I'm sure he's fine, Joseph," April said, giving him a sharp look, and nodding a bit toward Rose. "Let's not jump to conclusions.

"Nobody knows where he is," Joseph said. "It's been days. Something is wrong."

A few minutes later, a knock came at the door. The two cops standing outside were familiar. Bielby and Dunford. The state troopers. During their first visit, they'd acted, as cops do, mostly bored and detached, uninterested, it seemed, in listening to what April or Rose had to say. They would crack jokes and go through the motions slowly. They would do the bare minimum, just enough to record something in their files, and then they were gone. There was never any follow-up, and never, as far as April knew, any real progress. There had been a time when April wasn't sure how to interpret this indifference on the part of the police: was it confidence or overconfidence? Was it because they knew exactly what they were doing or was it what it looked like—complete incompetence? Whatever the case, April had long regarded these cop conversations as useless.

But now there was a different attitude altogether. They seemed alert and engaged. They were not cracking jokes, not taking their time. And on this occasion they were curt. April did not like the hostile looks they were giving her.

"Where is Rose?" Bielby said when April answered the door.

"She's in the bathroom," Joseph said.

The cop was already looking past April, into the house. He scooted past her and walked in.

"Excuse me," April said. "You can't just walk in here like that."

But he was already in. And when April turned to follow him, the other cop, Dunford, also entered. Both immediately got to snooping. They put a foot under the rugs and lifted them to look underneath. They tapped on the walls in particular spots. Bielby looked over the fireplace and began writing notes and taking pictures. He called his partner over, pointed next to the fireplace, then scribbled again in his notebook. A few more cops suddenly streamed in.

"Excuse *me!*" April said. "What is going on here?"

April marched over to the cops. Joseph, who'd tried to grab her, was too late to stop her. "What are you doing?" she said. "You can't just barge in here like this."

One of the cops, without even looking at April, put his hand into a pocket of his vest, pulled out a sheaf of paper, and held it up for April to take. She opened it and saw "Warrant for Home Search" written on top. Her eyes scanned the page. *Person of Interest*, it said. *Suspicion of Harboring a Fugitive*.

"Are you kidding me?" April said. "Is this always how you treat victims?"

"Let's talk this over," Joseph said to the cops.

But they ignored both of them and continued looking around the room.

Finally, one of them turned to April and said, "So where is she?"

"She doesn't have to talk to you," April said.

The cop pointed to the paperwork in April's hand.

"Judge disagrees, honey," he said. "This is what's gonna happen now. We're gonna execute this warrant. We're gonna look around, we're gonna gather some evidence. You got nothing to hide, you got nothing to worry about. Real simple. And we need to talk to Rose right now. We could do that here, or we could do that down at headquarters."

"She doesn't have to talk to you."

"True," the cop said. "And if she wants to exercise her right to remain silent, she can do that in a cell tonight. But it's just gonna make things drag out longer. Is that what we want?"

"It's fine," Rose said, as she drifted down the stairs. "I'll talk to them."

"Rose! Go back upstairs. I'm handling this," April said.

"Nah, I got it," Rose said. "They're right. I got nothing to hide. And it looks like they're finally ready to get serious and do their jobs. So let's talk."

Rose walked over to the kitchen counter, poured herself a cup of water, and sat down at the kitchen table.

"So what do ya wanna know?" she said, looking at the cops.

"No!" April said to Rose. "I'm asking the questions right now. What is the meaning of this?" she said, waving the document at the cops. "*Person of Interest?* For what?"

Dunford ignored April and pulled up a seat at the kitchen table across from Rose.

"Do you know a Micah Adam Brunwelder?"

"Yes," Rose said.

"What is your relationship to him?"

"I'm his great-aunt," Rose said.

"Just answer the question," Dunford said.

"I don't know," Rose said. "He's a guy. He's a friend.

I'm just getting to know him. He comes around here sometimes, to work on building projects with Joseph."

"Is he your boyfriend?" Bielby said.

Rose laughed.

"You can't be serious," she said. "I don't know. Not really. I think you know when someone is your boyfriend. So . . . no?"

"How long have you been together?"

"*We're not together.*"

"How long have you been not together?"

"A few months. Maybe, like three?"

"Do you tell each other things? Things of a private nature?" Bielby asked.

"Do you confide in each other?" Dunford added.

"Not really," Rose said. "No."

"Yes or no."

"No."

"Do you know where he is right now?"

"No, I don't. Haven't seen him since . . ." Rose said.

"When's the last time you saw him?"

"Are you gonna let me talk? I haven't seen him in . . . at least a week or so."

"And what did he tell you when you last spoke?"

"I don't know. He was talking about some building thing he was working on somewhere. . . ."

"Where?"

"I don't remember. I space out when he talks about that stuff."

"Where were you last Wednesday night?"

"Um, I don't know," Rose said, looking at April, who was shaking her head continuously. "Probably right here? I would have to think about it."

"Think about it," Dunford said.

Just then, Rose and April saw two plainclothesmen coming down the stairs. One was holding a moving box, the other was balancing a stack of Rose's notebooks.

"Hey, what are they doing!" April said. "Who are those guys?"

"They're detectives. They're taking a bunch of your things for analysis."

"You can't do this!"

"Once again," Bielby said, pointing to the papers in April's hands. "We have a search warrant. Do you have any computers that you use regularly?"

"No," Rose said.

"A phone?" Dunford asked.

"Yes," Rose said.

"We'll be taking that," he said. "Don't worry. You'll get it back. Long as you didn't do anything."

"Why are you doing this to me?"

Bielby gave her a curious look.

"Why do *you* think we're here?"

"I don't know," Rose said.

"If there's something you need to know, just ask it already," April said. "Get what you need here and leave. Is this how you treat everyone who's the victim of a crime?"

Dunford gave April a sharp look.

"Not another word out of you," he said, "or we're taking her in for questioning."

"Where were you last Wednesday night?" Dunford said.

"I was here," Rose said, composing herself. "We'd gone into town that day. But then I came back with Joseph in the afternoon and was here for the rest of the night."

"Here, in this house?"

"Yes."

"That's not what your boyfriend tells us," Dunford said.

"Did you see Micah that night?" Bielby added.

"No," Rose said.

"We're getting some contradictory stories here," Dunford said to one of the detectives, who was taking notes.

"I did see him that week, though," Rose said.

"Now we're getting somewhere," Bielby said. "Were you alone?"

"Yes," Rose said as she looked over at April. "We met in the forest out here. We had a picnic."

"Well, isn't that nice," the cop said.

"But that was Monday or Tuesday," Rose said. "Wednesday was the day I was in town. I know that. And I didn't see him that day."

The cops exchanged glances.

"What did he tell you?" Dunford said. "During your little picnic?"

"Not much. I don't remember," Rose said. "Just chitchat."

Rose remembered how Micah had looked that day. Somehow, next to the big maple trees, he looked even bigger himself. But he had laid out the picnic so gently, so carefully, that Rose had laughed. He'd clearly put a lot of thought into all the little foods he'd brought. Even his conversation had seemed a bit prepared, and Rose thought it most endearing. Had there actually been something off about his behavior? What could he have been hiding? Whatever it was, he must have been hiding it rather well.

"Rose," Bielby said. Both Rose and April bristled at hearing her name spoken by this man. "You need to tell us the truth. Lying to us right now will be really bad. For *you*. You understand?"

"I do," she said.

"Great," Dunford said. "Glad we all understand each other. Now I want you to think hard for a moment. Go back to that picnic. Was there anything Micah said or did that was odd?"

Rose thought about it. But she'd already been thinking about it and had come up with nothing that would be of any interest to the police.

"No, I'm telling you. There was nothing."

"We *know* that you know, Rose," Dunford said.

"Know what?"

"Do you know who Caroline Miller is?" Dunford asked.

Rose thought for a moment. The name did somehow sound vaguely familiar. But no, she didn't know anyone named Caroline.

"I don't know that name," she said.

"My partner is being nice about this," Dunford said. "The fact is we know what happened. Micah told us. Micah told us everything. He confessed. It's over, Rose. Your best option now is to confess, too. We know you were trying to help this girl. We know that you were trying to save her. We know you got caught up with a bad guy here. That's why we're not gonna arrest you. At least not yet. But we need your full cooperation right now, okay? We need you to tell us everything you know. Get it now?"

"Micah . . . *confessed?*"

"Does that surprise you?" Bielby asked.

"I have no idea what he would have to confess," Rose said. "I have no idea what any of you are talking about."

The cops exchanged another look.

"Last night your friend Micah confessed to the murder of Caroline Miller."

Chapter Sixteen

Rose was gripped by a deep chill.

"That's impossible," she said to the cops. "You're lying."

"No, we're not, kid," Bielby replied. "Your friend confessed to the murder of Caroline Miller. You know what else he said? Very interesting stuff. He said *you* knew about it before it happened."

"No, he didn't!"

"Oh, that's interesting," Bielby said. "You're not saying it's untrue . . . you're saying you don't think he *told* us. . . . Those are two very different things."

"Are you telling me," Dunford cut in, "that when we look at those notebooks over there, there won't be anything in there about Caroline Miller?" He suddenly turned angry. "'Cause we've got a murdered girl here. A girl with her neck *slashed* . . ."

"Stop it right now!" April shouted, and took a step toward Bielby. "Enough of this." Dunford grabbed her hard and held her back.

"We've got a young woman who's dead," Bielby began again, more deliberately. "We've got a suspect who's got her DNA *all over* his clothes. We have him on camera a few times. And . . . he confessed. He *confessed*. And we've got you, his girlfriend, who somehow knew for the past few weeks that something bad was going to happen to this girl. So now, you tell me. How should I interpret all of this?"

"I didn't know anything, and I didn't do anything wrong."

"Listen, hon. That's up to a judge to decide. We could arrest you right here. We have almost enough to charge you with accessory to murder. And I'm ready to bet that whatever is in those notebooks is not going to help your case. Now, you wanna know the truth? We don't wanna charge you. We know you've had a hard time recently. And you've helped us on the Whitey manhunt, told us about that note and the base he maintained in the area."

"Haven't helped too much, actually. It was the sister who told us about the note," one of the detectives suddenly said in the background. "Which is kinda interesting . . ."

"So, look, you got two options here. One, you confess. Tell us everything. And we won't arrest you. And if you do get charged with something, we'll make sure it's light. The other option is we arrest you, charge you with accessory, and probably a few other things, and let the prosecutor pick you apart. It's your choice."

Rose suddenly remembered something. Carly had recently come to Rose's window. Again. Rose should have been scared, but instead, again, her presence was reassuring. She had so much she wanted to ask Carly. And now here she was. Rose went to the window and opened it. She did it gently, so as not wake anyone in the house.

And also not to startle Carly, who seemed to be almost leaning into the window. When Rose opened the window and could view Carly more clearly, she saw lines on her face, bags under her eyes. She looked sleep deprived.

"Hi," Rose whispered.

"Rose," Carly said. "I'm close by."

"What do you mean?" Rose said. "You're right *here*." But Carly was gone.

Rose woke up from this dream, and she heard Carly's voice in her room. Maybe she was still a bit asleep. Maybe her sleep life was bleeding into her real life. But she thought she was awake and she distinctly heard Carly's voice in her room. And it said: "Tell them, Rose. When they come to you. Tell them what they want to hear."

"What's it gonna be?" said Bielby, staring at her with his dead, cop eyes.

"I've got nothing to confess to," she replied. "But I will answer all of your questions."

"Attagirl," Dunford said.

Chapter Seventeen

The cops seated Rose at a desktop computer.

"Why do all of your computers look like they're from 1998?" she said, as one of them searched for a file. "Do you guys have Internet on these things?"

The cops ignored her. Every time she looked up, she saw more cops. Cops walking in, and walking out. Cops seemed to be emerging from under desks to give her a look and then disappear. She did her best to keep calm.

"You know the bad guys have all the latest computers, right?" she said.

They continued to ignore her. One of the cops found the file and clicked on it. It was a grainy surveillance video. Rose fell silent.

Micah could be seen loading what looked like a large tarp into the trunk of a car. He went back and forth to that trunk loading supplies. It was definitely Micah. She recognized his big body. The surprisingly agile way he moved, the way he seemed to glide when he walked.

For a quick moment, his face passed near the camera and was visible. It was his face, no question about it. But the look on that face gave Rose pause. It wasn't a look she had seen before on him. It was a tense, blank look. His features seemed squeezed together. Somehow it just didn't seem like Micah. Was it him?

One of the cops paused the video. He tapped on the screen, at Micah's hand.

"There's the murder weapon," he said. "We have it here."

He pulled a large paper envelope out of a drawer. It had a tag on it that said SEALED EVIDENCE DO NOT TAMPER. He also produced a photo of a hammer.

"God, the jury's gonna love that," one cop said.

"Absolute beauty," said the other.

"Look familiar?" the first cop said to Rose, holding the photo of the hammer out toward her.

She knew immediately that it was Micah's favorite hammer. Or at least, that it looked exactly like the handmade, iron hammer he carried with him to every work site.

All at once, Rose felt deflated.

"So," said the cop, as he placed the envelope and photo back into the drawer, "are you starting to get the picture here? Micah did this crime. I know it seems crazy to you. Or maybe it doesn't, and maybe you knew about it all along. Whatever you knew or didn't know, and we're gonna talk all about that soon, I want you to understand, right now, that the case against Micah is rock solid. We got drawers and drawers of evidence here. He did this."

Rose said nothing. She shrugged.

"Listen, kid, he confessed, okay?" said another cop, and he pressed "Play" on another computer.

All of a sudden, Rose could hear Micah speaking. He sounded tired. He spoke much more slowly than she'd ever heard him speak. But it was his voice.

. . . *Yes, we brought her into that field*—there was a jump in the audio—*I was there. I was there all day*. ". . . you said you were there—where is 'there'? You're talking about the field where Caroline Miller was killed?" *Yes, in that field*. "And you were there for the sole reason of killing her?" There was a pause and some cross-talking. *Yes, I was there for that reason, to kill Caroline Miller*. "So I'm gonna ask this directly: Did you kill Caroline Miller?" There was some cross-talking. And then the cop said, "I'm going to ask you again. Were you directly involved in killing Caroline Miller?" On the recording, Micah paused for a long while. But the audio was still recording, as evidenced by the sounds of chairs moving, and shifting bodies. There was no audio cut here. Just a continuous recording from the question until Micah could be heard clearing his throat and finally saying, *Yes, I was*. "And the blood that was found on your clothes, and on your hammer . . . that was the blood of Caroline Miller?" *Yes, it was*, Micah said.

The officer pressed "Stop" on the recording.

"Do you believe us now?" he said. And when she did not reply, he added, "I could play you more if you want."

Rose shook her head slowly and looked down.

"What do you need from me?" she said quietly.

"We want to know how you knew the girl."

"Okay," Rose said. She looked up from the floor finally, directly at the cop. "You want me to believe you, that Micah kill—did this horrible thing. You want me to believe that? Fine. I believe you. But then I need you to believe me, too."

"We can try that," the cop said.

"I need you to believe me when I tell you I don't know who Caroline Miller is. I'd never heard that name until one of you said it. I never spoke to Micah about her; he never spoke to me about her. That's the truth."

"You know what?" the cop said. "I do believe you. I believe you think you're telling the truth. So let's try this a different way."

He reached into a file folder that was on the table and pulled out a portrait photo. He placed it on the table. He pointed to it.

"Do you know this person?"

Rose froze. She definitely knew this person. But who was it? She leaned in closer.

"I think I do," Rose said. "She's not someone I know well. But . . . she's so familiar."

"She's been missing for over a year," the cop said. He pulled out another piece of paper. It was a MISSING poster with the young woman's face on it.

"We don't want you remembering her face from the poster, so we showed you a different photo first," the cop said. "But it's still possible that you remember her from the poster. They've been all around for a while now."

"No," Rose said. "I don't know her from the poster. I know her from life."

The face was younger and fuller than the face of the person she remembered. But it was definitely the same.

"Carly," Rose heard herself say. She wasn't planning on saying her name, but it just slipped out of her mouth.

"Carly?" said the cop and gave a quick glance at his partner, who was sitting by the door. "Carly . . . what?"

"I don't know her last name," Rose said, thinking hard.

"How about Miller?" the cop said. "Carly Miller."

"Could be," Rose said.

"How did you know Carly?"

Rose looked directly at the cop who'd asked her this. She stared at him.

"As you know, I was abducted by Whitey Hornung," Rose said. "I met her in his compound. She was there, too."

There was sudden interest from some of the cops. They exchanged looks.

"Why didn't you mention this before?"

"Nobody asked."

"Did Micah ever talk to you about Carly?"

"Never."

"Did you talk to Micah about Carly?"

"Yes."

"Well, what did you say?"

"The truth is . . . I'd forgotten about her."

Tears suddenly and unexpectedly welled up in Rose's eyes. She fought them. She wasn't going to cry here. One of the cops slid a tissue box across the table until it hit Rose's hand.

"Go on. . . ."

"I promised her I'd never forget about her. But I did. I guess it was part of, I don't know, putting that whole thing behind me. But then she came to me. In a dream, I guess. She came to me at night. I saw her so clearly. As clearly as I see you here. And this happened a few times. And it shook me, obviously. Especially because it wasn't like a one-time thing. She just kept showing up."

"She must have said something to you. What was it? What did she say?"

"Nothing that I could understand. But I did sense that she was in distress somehow. And so she was on my mind, you know? That's why I mentioned it to Micah, the encounters. I told him about seeing her. And, to explain it, I told him about my experiences with her, when I was—when we were—together in Whitey's compound."

"Did you talk to anyone else about this?"

"No."

"Just Micah."

"Yes, just him."

"Why only him?"

"I can't talk to my sister about this kind of thing. It upsets her."

"And what did he say, when you told him about seeing this person?"

"Nothing much," Rose said. "He mostly just listened. And tried to be sympathetic about it, about how it was upsetting me to see her."

"Why was it upsetting?"

"I don't know where to start," Rose said. "We were both in this, like, cult together. I was there against my will. She was, too, I believe. I didn't really understand that at the time. I do now. Probably all the girls were there against their will. Anyway, I got out. It was a horrible experience. But I got out. I left her behind. I felt guilty about that, I guess. Mostly just really sad and scared for her. So, yeah, it was upsetting for many reasons."

"Did Micah ever mention that he knew her?"

"No," Rose said. "Why would he say that?"

"Because it's *true*," the cop said. "Micah knew her. They dated for years."

"*What?*" Rose put her hands over her face and squeezed her eyes closed. She opened them again rapidly and looked directly at the police officer who was sitting across from her. He looked sleepy, barely wore any expression at all.

"That's why he killed her, Rose. They knew each other well. They dated. She broke it off with him when he was having a hard time . . ."

". . . When his sister was killed . . ." another officer added.

"Right, it was right around that time. I dunno, maybe she couldn't handle that. Maybe he changed too much. They were pretty young. But she broke up with him during that period, and it wrecked the guy. He never forgave her. We believe that was the motive in this crime. And we don't just believe it. We have evidence to support it. It was an angry ex thing."

Rose was stunned. Her head was spinning. She didn't know what to say. Even if she had, she wouldn't have been able to speak. She was too shocked to get the words out.

"So what do you need from me?" she asked meekly.

"Well, we could use more evidence," the cop said.

His partner added, "And we still have some big unanswered questions—"

"We'd like to know what you knew, and when you knew

it," another cop interrupted. "We want to know whether to charge you for accessory."

"I didn't know anything about this," Rose said. "You need to believe me."

"Didn't you speak to Micah about her, just days before Micah killed her?"

"I guess so," Rose said. "But I didn't know that he knew her. I don't think either of us realized that we both knew her."

"Pretty big coincidence there," one of the cops said.

"It is true that Rose calls the victim Carly and everyone else knew her as Caroline," one of the other cops put in. "It's possible that she could talk about a Carly and he wouldn't think twice about it."

"So all of this is just an incredible coincidence?" one of the cops said, turning back to Rose. "You just happen to be chatting about this random person that you both knew . . . and then a few days later he murders her?"

"I don't know," said Rose. "But I do know, without a doubt, that I didn't realize that he knew her. And I had no idea that he was planning to . . . do something to her."

"But you said you knew she was in danger?"

"I sensed it. In my dreams, or whatever they were, she was telling me that she was in danger."

"Also a coincidence?"

"I mean, look, I met her when we were both kidnapped. I only knew her when she was in danger. But I didn't know she was in danger because of anything Micah told me. If he did something . . ."

"It's not 'if' . . . we *know* he did. He confessed. There's evidence. . . ."

"Fine," she said. "Whatever he did was something I had

no idea about. Not before it happened, and not after. This is the first I've heard about it. You have to believe me."

"You know what," the cop said, suddenly changing his tone. "I do believe you. You know why? I got a theory. Why don't you tell me what you think of this?"

He looked at her for a long moment, and she realized he was asking her a question.

"Uh, okay," she said. "What's your theory?"

"Thought you'd never ask," he said. "But before we get to that, I have another question for you. I can tell that you still think Micah is innocent. And it's sweet, in a way. But it also makes me wonder if you're covering for him. But let's put that aside for a moment. Let's go with your belief: Micah didn't do this. So who do you think did it?"

"How would I know? I have no idea who the killer was."

"But you knew Carly. You know something about her. Given what you know, who would you guess might harm her? If not Micah?"

"Well, Whitey. He kidnapped her. You were looking for her for a year. She shows up dead. Wouldn't the kidnapper be your first suspect? I can tell you, for a fact, that Whitey was the one holding her against her will."

"Right! Exactly. Whitey has to be behind this, right?"

"Right," Rose said, unsure of what she was agreeing to.

"But here's the thing about that," the cop said. "Your friend Micah? He *worked* for Whitey."

"No," Rose said, involuntarily.

"He did, kid. We know this. We know it because we had him on tape during one of Whitey's deals. We were even trying to get to him, make him an informant for us. There are things about your friend that you didn't know. Unless you do and you're not telling us."

Rose said nothing. She just stared at the table, trying to process this information.

"Obviously Micah's involvement with Whitey shapes how we see this case. It could explain a lot. It explains how he got access to that girl. It explains why, too. At some point, Whitey wanted this girl gone. And Micah was just the person to do it. Maybe even the person to take the fall for it. Micah helped Whitey solve this problem."

"It also explains you," said another cop. "It explains why Micah got so friendly with you."

"What does *that* mean?"

"He knew that you knew the girl. He was curious to learn what you knew about her. He was using you to get more information about her. Or maybe just to, I don't know, get news about her."

"So what do you want from me?" Rose said.

"We don't understand why he killed her when he did," the cop said. "We think we have a motive: he felt betrayed by her, he wanted revenge. But why now? And how did it happen that she ended up in his custody?"

"How would I know?"

"You know more than you realize."

"I think I know less than *you* realize," she said.

"We want to know what Micah told you."

"I don't have the answers you want," Rose said. "Maybe you should ask Micah."

The cops looked at each other.

"Well," one of them said, "funny you should say that because we were hoping you would ask him for us."

"Look," the other cop said, "if you don't help us here, we'll have to assume you're covering for him. In that case, we're gonna charge you with accessory, if not more. You'll do years in state. It's up to you."

Chapter Eighteen

It rained nonstop for three days. And these three days were, it seemed, the first days in a long while that Carly didn't visit her. But she was very much on Rose's mind. And so was Micah. Stuck at home, inside all day, Rose had plenty of time to think. She would sit by the window and watch the rain alternating between torrential and misty, watching the sudden newly formed rivulets rushing across the field in front of the barn, and down into the fields and the forest beyond. For a moment, she thought she saw someone in the forest. A quick flash of movement. But it was probably nothing. Who would possibly be out there now?

She was trying to imagine Micah and Carly together as a couple. The image seemed crazy to her. These people came from such different parts of her life. In retrospect, though, these parts of her life weren't that far apart at all. And Micah and Carly were, in the end, both from similar Amish communities. Their being together made more sense than Micah and Rose. Still, she was having a hard time imagining them together. What did they talk about? What did they argue about? What was it like when they broke up? She could imagine them clashing. She could even imagine Micah murdering her.

The thought startled her. She'd never taken him to be violent. Or vindictive. If you'd told her a month ago that Micah had committed a murder, she would have laughed at the suggestion. And when the cops had said it to her, she'd immediately rejected the notion as absurd. But the evidence was undeniable. And the evidence forced her to confront what Micah had done to this girl and also what she herself knew about Micah all along, but denied: that he could be emotional, maybe even unhinged. A bit unpredictable, impulsive. His charisma could be very alluring. But wasn't it often also the sign of someone with an excess of energy, someone who was, after all, aggressive toward others? His need to be loved and admired made him sometimes a bit desperate and manipulative.

She'd seen little flashes of anger in him. He'd once suggested to her that they hunt Whitey down. They'd been standing in the barn together as she fed the horses. He talked about his plan to take vengeance on Whitey for her.

"The police won't do what needs to be done," he'd said to her.

He'd lifted a big rusty hook, which they used around the barn for various things. "I could do more with this hook than those guys ever would with their little notebooks and badges."

At the time, Rose had dismissed this talk. In his sincerity and his passion to defend her, it was even kind of winning. He cared about her. He wanted to harm those who had harmed her. He wanted to exact revenge for her. This was not without appeal to her. Even as it was happening, though, she did push back a bit and say, "Well, you *could* just use a gun, you know?" And she had noted his reply: "He doesn't deserve a gun. He deserves a hook." But even in that moment, when she smiled at this talk and even goaded him on by saying "Are you trying to flirt with me now?" some part of her noted that his talk had crossed a line. She had tucked all of this away with a little red flag on it. A man picking up a big rusty hook and fantasizing about using it against another person . . . well, it was just a bit off. Now that she'd learned what he'd done, she wanted to be shocked. But she wasn't.

She was, however, disappointed—in herself. Disappointed that she'd ignored her own judgment, turned a blind eye to her own raised red flags. She'd let this guy into her life. And worse. If the cops were right that Micah had worked for Whitey, that he was part of that world, she'd let some of that darkness back into her life, just when she thought she'd escaped it.

She looked out at the rain, which had picked up again. She opened the window a crack, letting in some of the mist and also the pleasant din of rainfall. It was possible that she'd caught a big break now that Micah was locked away. What had happened to Carly was too awful to even contemplate. But it could have been her, too. She could have been with this guy. And then, one day, he might have turned on her. She could have quickly become the one he turned his violence against, instead of the one he defended. And she could easily have been another one that they were burying. Their relationship could have ended under much worse circumstances for her. She had to be grateful that he was locked up.

When the rain had finally passed on the third night,

Rose was eager to get out of the house. After a sunny morning, the fields had dried somewhat, and Rose decided to make a trip into the woods. After three days of rain, there would be so much to forage. She could harvest enough mushrooms to use for weeks. More importantly, she could get out of the house, out of her head, out of her fears.

The forest smelled delicious to her. The soil was so fresh, its rich and nourishing aromas lifted Rose slightly off her feet. She felt a surge of oxygen in her blood, in her brain. She was suddenly fully alert, alive. Every sense was sharpened. Even her extra senses were heightened. She could sense the trees around her bursting with energy, could almost feel them taking big deep drinks of ground water, and conveying it deep into their wooden veins. The ground itself felt alive and new and buoyant.

Nothing else mattered to her. She was fully in the moment in that forest. Everything else was just sleepwalking. Every conversation was just mumbling underwater. *This* was her life. This alertness, this pool of oxygen that lifted her up a foot off the forest floor, this was her truest life.

As she'd expected, the mushrooms were plentiful. She barely needed to scout for them. She could pretty much walk along the path and merrily scoop up mushrooms every few steps, tossing them into her basket. She even passed up a few that were a bother to reach, something she would usually not do. But today the forest was generous and she was basking in its abundance.

Rose was feeling too high, too open and relaxed, to register the sudden, unexpected presence standing between two trees. It was Carly.

"Hi," Rose said. "You can't be real."

Carly just looked at her. In the shade of the trees, the color of her face, her brown eyes, glowed. If this was a figment, it was a remarkably vivid one.

"Rose," Carly said, in little over a whisper. "I can't stay long."

"Where are you going? They say you're dead. Are you?"

"Rose," Carly said. "Don't ask questions right now. I don't have a lot of time. So just listen to my message: Whitey has done more for you than you know."

"What are you talking about?"

"No questions, dear. I need to go now."

"What? No, don't!" Rose said, suddenly lurching toward Carly. "I need to know if you're even real. I need to understand what you mean."

"There's no time to explain," Carly said. "Just listen to me. Whitey wants to let you know that it's going to be okay. And that he wants to meet with you. To explain. He will come to you."

"No, I want *you* to come to me! Or just *stay*. Stay! I have so many questions!"

"No," Carly said. "He will come, he will answer you. And if you listen to him . . . I might be able to come back to you. You are safe now that Micah is away."

"What are you saying?"

Carly turned away.

"No, wait!" Rose said. "Stop!"

But Carly was already walking quickly through the forest.

"Stop!" Rose said again and quickened her pace to catch up with Carly. Soon they were both running through the woods. Carly seemed to be moving effortlessly. And she pulled away. At just that moment, Rose tripped on a branch and fell hard into a ditch under a large fallen tree trunk. She could immediately feel her knee swelling up, blood trickling down her ankle. With a lot of effort, she wriggled herself into a sitting position, pulled herself up onto a branch, and looked around. Carly had vanished.

Rose had no idea how she'd gotten home. She'd been farther into the forest than she'd ever gone. She was very nearly lost. And if she hadn't broken a bone in her leg, it certainly felt as though she had. But somehow, by instinct and sheer will, she dragged herself back through the woods and ended up back at home.

"Where on earth have you been?" April shouted the second she walked in. "And wait, omigod, what *happened* to you?"

April ran to Rose.

"Thank God you're okay," she said as she threw her arms around her. "Let's get you cleaned up."

They sat in Rose's room for a long fifteen minutes without saying a word to each other. Rose had taken a shower, and April had helped her put bandages on her leg. They sat on her bed and said nothing. It was obvious that April wanted to talk but she waited to let Rose say the first word. The silence between them was so complete that when Rose opened her mouth to speak, April immediately looked over toward her, even before she'd made a sound.

"I just," Rose said. "I dunno. I dunno what to say."

"Maybe we should move," April said. "I still believe

we're safe here. And I'm not one to let people scare me. But maybe I'm lying to myself. Maybe we should come up with a plan to . . ."

"Nah," Rose said. "I don't think it matters where we go. He'll just find me there."

"Don't say that, Rosie."

Rose told her about Carly. That she'd come to her in the woods. That she'd talked to her about Micah, told her it was good he was in jail. And that Carly talked to her about Whitey.

"Rose," April said. She paused to choose her words carefully. "Rose, Carly . . . is dead."

"She seemed pretty real," Rose said. "And anyway, how do we know she's dead? They haven't found her body."

"The video . . ."

"It's not clear, Ri. If you think about it, we're taking the cops at their word here."

"Okay, but even if she were alive. You think she's just gonna appear like this?"

Rose didn't reply. Then she shrugged.

"Well, what did Carly say to you about Whitey?"

Rose turned to April.

"She said . . . she said that Whitey wants to see me."

April laughed. Rose gave her a quizzical look.

"Sorry. But . . . *what?* He wants to *see* you? What does that even mean? Is that exactly what she said?"

"Well, she said 'meet.' He wants to meet with me."

"Okay, that's just crazy. After all of this, he wants to . . . *meet* with you? Like to catch up over coffee?"

"Maybe I should do it."

"Why would you do that?"

"To get him off my back. To get the cops off my back."

"What do the cops have to do with this?"

"They want me to talk to Micah. But maybe I should do them one better and talk to Whitey. Get some real answers."

April shook her head.

"No, no, no," April said. "No way."

But Rose had already made up her mind.

Chapter Nineteen

Rose wanted to see Micah again. She had her own questions for him. She wanted to look him in the eye when he answered her. She decided that she needed to talk to him again. For herself, not just the cops. And just once. To finally get some answers. And the moment she made this decision, she realized that she would never see him again. Because even though she was nearly obsessed with getting the answers she needed, answers that only he could give her, she knew she could never visit him in a prison. And he would never leave that prison. She knew that. And she also knew, as she never had quite before, that she was not capable of entering a prison.

She called the prison up and asked if visitors had to "go into the part of the prison that is locked" and the officer who answered the phone just laughed at her. After her time as Whitey's captive, there was nothing that could persuade her to purposely enter a prison.

But she couldn't stop thinking about Micah. Not about Micah himself, but the questions that Micah might be able to answer. About Carly. About Whitey. And about

Rose herself. Micah was the thread that connected them all. And he knew things that he hadn't told Rose. He'd lied to her.

Why? The simple reason seemed to be that he was hiding something from Rose. Or that he wanted something from her. The case against Micah seemed undeniable. She'd seen the surveillance videos. She'd heard his own voice confess. Just because the cops were cocky didn't mean they were wrong. She needed to see Micah. To hear him say it to her.

But she delayed. She couldn't stand the thought of walking into a prison, seeing and especially hearing the steel prison locks closing behind her. Just the thought of that was enough to keep her up at night. It was the same fear, too, that made her want to cooperate with the police. Her biggest fear was that her terror of prison would lead her to tell the police anything they wanted to hear. Anything to avoid winding up there herself.

April's friend and mentor, Carmen, had hired a lawyer for Rose, to keep her out of legal trouble now that Micah was facing charges. Every few days, Rose would sit on the steps to the porch and pet Darlene and throw her sticks to fetch as a chatty Center City Philadelphia lawyer named Katherine held forth over the phone.

"I wouldn't visit him," she told Rose on one of these calls. "Hard to imagine what good could come of it. And I could think of some *bad* things. Weird optics, that's for sure. Definitely could go south. I mean, guess it wouldn't be the worst thing to find out what his counsel is planning on using as a defense. Wouldn't mind knowing *that*. But don't ask directly. And I'm not advising you to go. I'm just saying *if* you go, ask . . ."

The lawyer didn't finish the sentence.

"Oh, okay," Rose said abruptly. "I think I understand." She tossed a stick again toward the barn, sending Darlene galloping after it.

"Honestly, it's probably best to just skip it. You know what I mean? Less risky. But if you go, do it soon. Because once the trial begins, you can*not* have any contact with him. Especially if you end up being a witness in this case, which is very possible. That's an absolute no-no. And like I said, even now, pretrial, you're pushing it."

"Would I be able to see him again, like, after the trial?"

"After you testify *against* him?"

"Wait, what?"

Rose could hear a sigh over the line.

"Yeah, listen, we haven't discussed all of this yet. But here's a preview: that's what the prosecution is gonna demand that you to do. They're gonna want you to testify. And they're basically gonna pressure you into it by threatening to throw the book at you if you don't. It's a good idea to play along for the most part. But you should also know that the threats are mostly bluff. It's BS, okay? They don't really have anything on you. Even if they had the audacity to charge you with accessory, or something like that, it would be a stunt. An intimidation tactic. It wouldn't stick. They know it. And I'll make sure of it. All that talk was just to shake you up because you were talking to them without a lawyer, which of course you won't do again, right?"

"Right," Rose said, standing up now to stretch her legs.

"We'll talk soon about testifying. Don't be worried about it! It's okay. It's normal. Happens all the time. It will be unpleasant and then it will be over. So, yeah, you will be called to testify, at least in writing. Possibly in open court. I'll try to get you out of that. But anyway, you are now working with the prosecution here, hon. So I'm not sure your friend is gonna *want* to talk to you again. But anyway, once the trial is done, once he's convicted and sentenced, you might be able to get a visit in, if that's something you both agree on. I mean, he'll have *plenty* of time for a visit, that's for sure." Katherine laughed hoarsely. Rose could hear her take a big sip of a drink.

"You seem pretty certain that he'll be convicted."

"I am certain, yes," the lawyer said. "Your friend will be convicted. He's toast."

Rose heard her take another big gulp of her drink.

"Oh, and just one more thing about that. There is also the question of an appeal. If he fights this and doesn't plead guilty—which, I have to tell you, would be a pretty bad decision on his part because he'll lose—then he will likely also make an appeal. If he does that, and especially if he does it right away, you might not be able to see him during that process either. Same as the trial. In that case, and depending on how that process is arranged, it could be a long time, years even. So, again, not telling you whether you should go or not. But if you want a visit with him, I'd do it right away."

Rose hitched a buggy ride with April and Joseph to Lancaster, right up to the door of the Lancaster County Prison. That's what it was called. None of the euphemisms like Department of Correction or Detention Center. The word *Prison* appeared right over the front gate. And it was indeed a gate. A giant wrought-iron arched gate set between two massive castellated turrets, a design that was immediately recognizable as a medieval castle. When the buggy turned on to East King Street, and she saw the castle prison, she couldn't help herself, she burst out laughing.

"What's so funny?" April asked from the front of the buggy.

"Just look at it," Rose said, leaning forward to get a better look. "It's just so . . . castle-y, like they're trying really hard or something."

As they drew closer, and the actual prison building behind the castle facade became visible, and as the razor wire that surrounded the compound came into focus, Rose got quiet again. She was beset by her earlier thoughts, her fear of entering a prison, of being closed in, completely at the mercy of those expressionless jailers.

Rose made her way laboriously through the prison. Into the lobby, where she filled out paperwork, through the security checkpoints, through the double doors that closed with a hellish clang, through the windowless concrete halls—whose echoes reminded her of Whitey's compound—and finally into the prison visiting area. The entire journey was made by her legs, but not quite her soul, which hovered overhead.

And then she saw him. She saw Micah, and suddenly her soul zipped back into her body, and her eyes suddenly came into focus, as though waking from a restful sleep. Here he was. He looked thinner than usual. The dark green jumpsuit he wore gave him the look of an airport tarmac technician rather than a prisoner. Rose slipped into her seat and grabbed the telephone receiver. He was already seated behind thick bulletproof glass, holding his own telephone receiver. She took a long look at him, at his familiar face. The smile, the dimples. It all came back at once.

"Rose," he said. "I can't believe it's really you."

Chapter Twenty

That night, Whitey came to Rose. She woke up in her bed in a sweat. She didn't know how, but she knew without any doubt that Whitey was in the house. She also felt as if nobody else was home. Everyone was gone. It was just the two of them in the house. Rose, in bed. Whitey . . . somewhere in the house. She climbed out of bed. Slowly. Trying not to make a sound. Trying not to let her feet creak the wooden floorboards. Once her feet were on the floor, she crouched down, feeling with her hand, under the bed, for the knife she'd bought for just this situation. Then she remembered the night the stranger had stayed over, the man she'd believed to be Whitey. How she'd planned to plunge that knife into his neck that night. But April had stopped her. And she'd taken the knife downstairs and stashed it under the kitchen sink, where it remained.

There was a sound downstairs. Whitey. Rose was certain of it. She heard him walking very slowly over the floorboards. So slowly that he could only have been doing it on purpose, so as not to be detected. Then she heard him start to climb the stairs that way, too. One foot on the first stair. Then silence. Then the next step. Then silence. She listened to him walk all the way up, right until he was standing in front of her door.

She threw it open. Nobody was there. She closed her eyes and opened them again. He was standing right there. She should have been afraid. But she was strangely calm.

"I'm not your sister," Rose said to him.

"Don't say that, dear," Whitey replied.

"I'm not your sister," Rose repeated.

"Is that any way to greet an old friend?" Whitey said.

"I'm not your sister," Rose said again.

"We can discuss all of that in due time," Whitey said. "Let's catch up first."

"How is this happening?" Rose asked.

"You know that I'm not here right now? I'm not in your room," Whitey said.

"I know that," Rose replied. "That's why I'm not nervous."

"You have nothing to be nervous about, dear," Whitey said. "Even if I was there."

"But you're not," she said.

"But I am real," he said. "And we are really talking. This isn't a dream. You know that, too, don't you?"

"Yes," Rose said. "I know that you're real. I know that we're talking. I know that I'm not asleep."

"Well, good then," Whitey said. "See how well we're getting along?"

"Everyone is looking for you," she said. "It's just a matter of time. You should just give up."

Whitey laughed.

"Is that what the cops told you?"

"No, actually they didn't," she said, "but that's what I think."

"Listen to me closely," he said. "What I'm about to tell you isn't just talk. It's reality. The sooner you hear this and understand it, the better. The police will never find me. Never. And anyway, the FBI knows where I am. And they're fine with it. I'm valuable to them. And I'm also dangerous to them. They don't want me talking in court. They don't want me to spill their secrets. I know things about them. It's very important that you understand something: I will not be caught by the police. It won't happen. If that's what you're hoping for, you should let it go it now."

"What have you done with Carly?"

"I don't know who that is," he said.

Rose gave him a long searching look. There was something opaque about his expression, not a thickness like a mask, but a thinness like a distorted image. She couldn't tell anything from it.

"Caroline," Rose said. "She was one of the girls . . . in the Community."

"Ah, yes, of course," he said. "She's fine. Why wouldn't she be? I know you're fond of her. That's why I sent her to you last week. Did she seem dead to you?"

"So it *was* you," Rose said.

"Of course it was," Whitey replied. "It's always me. You know that."

"And that strange man who came to this house, randomly that night, looking for food . . . was that you, too?"

"Yes," Whitey said. "It's always me."

"I mean, was that actually *you?*"

Whitey laughed.

"No! You thought that was *me?*"

"In disguise . . ."

"No, no," Whitey said. "But I did pay him to visit . . . to check on you and leave that note."

"And Carly . . . Caroline?"

"She's one of mine."

"If she's still alive . . . let her go, Whitey," Rose said.

"Do not call me that. Ever. How dare you use that name with me!"

A cold fear gripped Rose from behind, so quickly that she was certain it was a person grabbing at her. Even through the distorted expression on his face, she could see his eyes burning with rage. She could feel the fear, an old fear, squeeze at her throat.

"S-s-sorry," she said. "I didn't m-mean . . ."

"It's okay," he said with a clenched jaw. "Let's not dwell on it. Let's get back to what you said. You asked me about Caroline. You asked me to 'let her go.' She can go. She can leave anytime. I'm not keeping her. She came to me by her own choice; she stays with me by her own choice. I give her everything she needs. Everything she never got when she lived outside, in the fallen world. She's happy. I can send her to you again and you can ask her yourself."

"What do you want from me?" Rose asked.

"Are you really asking that?" he said.

"Yes, I am. Please tell me! I'll do it. I just want to be . . . free of this."

"You know what I want . . ." he said.

"*Rosie.*"

It was April. She was standing in the door. "Who are you talking to?"

"Nobody," she said to April. She looked toward Whitey, but he was nearly gone. Just a vague outline of him remained. She exhaled and suddenly realized that she'd been holding her breath. She was panting slightly and sweating.

"Rosie, are you okay?"

"I'm fine," she said.

April gave her a long look.

"I'm *fine*."

In the corner of her room, fading out, was an image of Whitey. She could hear him, just barely, saying, "*Hefsibah, Hefsibah,* I'll come back to you soon. . . ."

A few days later, Carly's body was found in a ravine. The police had determined that she'd been hastily buried nearby, but with the waters rising after the rains, her body was pulled from the shallow grave and eventually washed ashore, where it was discovered by a hunter.

Chapter Twenty-One

When Rose got to the Lancaster County Court—by buggy with Joseph and April—she was surprised to find a crowded courtroom. She hadn't thought about how many people might be there, or what drew them. But there they were. As she walked by, she studied their faces for any clue, for the reason why they might be there. But they seemed to have come just for entertainment. Just because they'd read about this case in the papers.

It had been a prolonged pretrial period. Getting a jury seemed to take forever as the attorneys haggled over each potential juror, and the defense tried to have the trial moved on the grounds that Micah couldn't get a fair trial in a small city where everyone knew everyone else. The judge did not agree. Now, after so much procedural haggling, the trial was set to begin.

And just then, almost hours after the trial date had finally been announced, it happened: the sensational discovery of the murder victim's body. This had been the big missing piece of evidence, the thing that the defense had pinned much of its hopes on (*How can someone be tried for murder when we don't even have a murder victim?*).

The body was the thing that now sealed the deal for the prosecution. To Rose, the news was crushing. She somehow hadn't believed it was really true. And now there could be no denying it: Carly was gone. The person she knew, the person who'd reached out to her and helped keep her sane during her kidnapping ordeal, was now dead. And the double blow was that Micah was the killer.

The mood in the courtroom on the first day was surprisingly celebratory. Those who knew Carly/Caroline were somber. You could tell who these people were. They looked stricken. But there weren't too many. Most people acted as if they were at a volleyball game. It was the kind of crowd that, once upon a time, would make a picnic to watch a hanging.

The day in court was long. There was a lot of waiting around, incoherent court chatter, and then opening arguments from the prosecution, which included a detailed litany of charges against Micah and a detailed account of how he'd committed the murder. Most of the information was not new to Rose. But there were a few new details. And she was sad and horrified to hear some of the account that she had supplied now used in court. To hear it all brought together and woven into such a damning narrative about Micah was demoralizing. How could anyone hear it and not feel certain that this man had killed a woman in cold blood? Rose, who barely knew what to believe anymore, was herself convinced. She reminded herself, for the millionth time, that there were clearly parts of Micah and his life that she didn't know.

Some part of her maintained the ability to question, though. Or maybe to hope. Or maybe it was just the capacity to delude herself. But it was precisely because her world was rocked by the trial, because all her assumptions about what she knew (and didn't know) were thrown out the window, that she held on to some hope. If Micah could prove to be a murderer, despite seeming to be a good person, was not the opposite also true? Was it not possible that he could be innocent even though everything pointed to his being a murderer? Rose could admit that the logic seemed too convenient. She wouldn't say anything like this to April; she wouldn't even admit to herself that she thought such things. But somewhere, deep down, she hoped.

But then the defense made its opening statements and outlined its arguments. And that was when Rose finally lost all hope. Where the prosecution was organized and specific, listing the time—sometimes down to the second—of the sequence of events, and listing evidence, the defense spoke in general terms and pointed to very little evidence. Even more troubling, the attorney told a story that seemed obviously made up. The whole defense seemed like a convenient web of excuses.

The defense started by agreeing with almost everything the prosecution had said about the timeline of events. Micah was indeed where they said he was, when they said he was there. He was at the scene of the crime. He was indeed caught on camera arriving and leaving. And yes, that blood on his clothes was the victim's blood. And yes, the murder weapon belonged to Micah. It was all true! But, said his attorney, he was forced to do these things. Two men were there with him. And they forced him, at gunpoint, to do all of these things. They set him up to look like the killer. They forced him to act as an accessory to the crime. When he was filmed packing blood-covered sheets into a car trunk, that really was him helping clean up the crime. But it wasn't his crime; the murder had been committed by these two men. Who were the men? He didn't know. He couldn't say. But these were people who wanted Carly dead. And wanted him to take responsibility.

Rose's heart fell when she heard this defense. Who would believe it? How would the attorney prove it? She doubted it herself. The story just didn't add up. And if even she didn't believe it, how would a jury be convinced? She remembered what her own lawyer had said: "He's toast."

That night she sat in front of the fire. She didn't feel like talking. But April kept asking her questions. April hadn't joined Rose because she had had her own bad experiences with courts and couldn't bring herself to ever enter a courtroom again. She also thought it was a bad idea for Rose to attend the trial. She felt that Rose should cut off all connection with Micah. And nothing good would come of her being in the courtroom. But she was also very curious to hear how the trial was going.

Rose told her how bad it was. How unconvincing the defense was, how ridiculous.

"People were literally laughing," Rose said.

"When court was in session?"

"When Micah's lawyer was going on about how there were these mystery men who forced Micah to clean up the murder scene . . . people broke out laughing."

"Are you sure?"

"Ri, yes," Rose said. "I'm sure. It wasn't quiet. It was like a lot of people suddenly laughing. The judge got mad and said, 'The next person who makes a disturbance will be escorted out of here.'"

"Yikes," April said. "Well, what do you think happened?"

"I don't know anymore," Rose said, picking up some small chips of wood that had fallen off the logs and throwing them into the fire.

"I mean the video is kind of crazy. It's just Micah. There are no other people in it."

"Maybe they planned it that way," April suggested.

"They?" Rose said. "Anyway, when he's putting the bloody sheets into the trunk, it really looks pretty convincing."

"Wait, *he's putting the bloody sheets into* . . . what did you say?"

"The trunk."

"The trunk? Like . . . of a car?" April asked.

"Yeah, it's like five minutes after the crime, and you can see the time stamp clearly in the video. The trunk's open and he's just loading it up with supplies. Including the sheets with this girl's blood all over it, and also the murder weapon. It doesn't look good."

"Yeah, but you said 'trunk.' Micah doesn't have a *trunk*. He doesn't have a car," April pointed out.

"He has a license, though," Rose said. "I remember because I asked him about Amish people and licenses. He told me he did it for work."

"Fine," April said. "But he doesn't have a car. So that car must belong to someone else. Someone else must be involved in this."

Rose didn't reply at first. They all watched the fire get hotter but smaller, condensed into embers.

"Ri," Rose said finally. "He confessed to the killing. And even when I visited him, he wouldn't deny it. I asked him straight out. I looked him right in the eyes."

Chapter Twenty-Two

That night, Whitey came to Rose. She had been outside, in the woods, sitting on a log, eyes closed, trying to commune with Carly. A few times, she was close. She could even see Carly's face. And hear her voice. But she couldn't make out a word. It was as though she were listening to someone speak underwater. And then she would disappear. Rose would try again, and it would happen again. Finally it stopped working altogether. The connection was so thoroughly gone, it was as though it had never existed. And for a moment Rose thought maybe it hadn't. Maybe all of these sessions, at night and during the day, had been mere flickers of imagination. Her trust in herself was wavering.

That's when Whitey came to her.

"How do I know it's really you? How do I ever know your visits aren't just dreams?"

Whitey seemed genuinely amused, and he laughed heartily.

"I'm almost complimented," he said, "that you think I'm a vision, that you think you might have dreamed me. Do you, Rose? Do you dream about me often?"

"Well," Rose said, "when you say weird creepy stuff like that . . . it does sound like you. What do you want?"

"That's rather a rude way to begin a conversation, isn't it?"

"I'll walk away," she said. "I owe you nothing."

"Ah," he said. "But I have something you want. So you'd be rather foolish to walk away."

"What is it? Just tell me. I don't want to play games."

"I have information about your friend Micah. So sad what's become of him, by the way."

"And what do you want in exchange?"

"I want to see you in person."

"And if I say no?"

"Micah stays in prison for the rest of his natural life."

"Are you honestly telling me you know something that will change the outcome of his trial?"

"So sad about Carly, isn't it? Very promising young woman. Do you think Micah could have gotten to her without my knowing something about it?"

"So what do you know about it?"

"Meet with me. I'll tell you."

"I'm meeting with you right now."

"You know what I want. You know it can only happen in person."

"I'm not meeting with you. Unless you tell me what this is about."

"Micah is not guilty," Whitey said.

"He confessed to the murder. There's evidence," she replied.

"Confessions are always partial truths. Evidence is play money. There's a reson why he changed the story and decided to plead 'not guilty.'"

"How do you know?"

"I make it my job to know things," he said. "Meet with me and I'll give you the details. I'll tell you how to get him out."

"I'll think about it," she said.

"Don't think too much about it," he said. "We will speak again. And you will let me know whether you want to save Micah's life or not."

A few days later, Rose got a text. It was from the public defender, the person who was representing Micah in court.

big turn in the case. can't go into detail here.
come to court Monday morning 9:00 A.M.

Rose wanted to text her back, but her phone died. And that meant she probably wouldn't be able to get back to the attorney until the next morning, when she would be able to get to town to charge the phone. But the message was clear enough. And she waited breathlessly, trying to imagine what it could mean. *Big turn in the case.*

Early Monday morning, she pestered Joseph to move faster, to get her to Lancaster in time. They made it there forty-five minutes early, and she waited outside the closed courthouse. She sat on the steps.

"I thought that was you," a woman said as she approached the steps. "I'm Casey. I'm serving as Micah's lawyer."

"Oh, hi!" Rose said, getting to her feet. "I've seen you in court."

"Yeah, I get that a lot. Listen, I couldn't say this over text, but there's some huge news here. A real bombshell. Usually I wouldn't be talking to you at all, much less about the trial, since you're technically on a list of potential witnesses for the prosecution, but I'll give you the goods because I know the prosecution bullied you into testifying and this trial is about to blow up."

"I know he's innocent," Rose said.

"Well, knowing is one thing, proving is another. But now we have corroborating witnesses. In fact, the two guys who actually committed this murder. They did it for Whitey. It was all him. But they were brought in on other charges and are in jail right now. One of them saw the news about this case and boasted about it to another inmate, who informed on him. The other one was also identified, though it's unclear to me how they knew it was him. Both were questioned and have agreed to cut a deal in this case, in exchange for dishing on Whitey, who is after all, the bigger fish, the one the cops are really after. So this trial with Micah? It's about to completely change. They're probably going to suspend the trial. They'll definitely drop the worst charges."

Rose just stared.

"I don't know what to say," Rose finally said. "Will he actually get out?"

"Yes," she said. "He'll walk right out these doors. Not today. But really soon."

Rose heard nothing for the next three days. After she'd met the lawyer on the steps, she'd skipped court. For the rest of that day, and the next and the next, she stayed home and kept herself busy. She tried not to get too excited about seeing him. For one thing, it might not happen at all. And even if he did get out, it didn't mean he would be eager to see her. They'd had a tense interaction during her prison visit. He knew that the prosecutor was considering putting her on the witness stand. He knew that she'd spoken to the police, and that the court had extracted a testimony from her. Maybe he didn't want to see her now. As the days went by, she gradually came to accept the fact that he was either not getting out of jail, or that he didn't want to see her. But the more she tried to temper her expectation of seeing him, the more she did precisely what she had been trying to avoid: she thought about him, about their time together, before everything changed.

The first time she'd really looked at Micah, the first time she really saw him, was during a family picnic at the farm. Micah had been there, along with his extended family. His parents, his brothers and sisters, his nieces and nephews. And especially the two nieces he was closest to: the daughters of his departed sister.

After her death, Micah and the girls had clung to each other. The story everyone told was that *he was there for them*. He was the children's rock. But Micah had later confided it was the opposite. That it was the children who had kept him sane. (And very possibly the only reason he wanted to continue living at all.) He'd told her that it scared him to think that these children, these short, bony little creatures, who had only begun to speak in sentences, could somehow hold that much power over him.

And when Rose was being honest with herself, she was also scared. She was scared of the power this flawed man had over her thoughts, her feelings. She sometimes didn't know what to make of him. He seemed to hoard attention. In social settings, he often took center stage. He could talk over people, ignore people. He didn't always, or maybe ever, read situations correctly. Or he didn't care. Either way, there was a problem. He was a performer. And a pleaser. He clearly loved his nieces . . . but also seemed to love the attention he got as the Good Uncle. He enjoyed that persona just a bit too much, didn't he? And he was hiding things about himself. Possibly he was hiding things even from himself. The range of possibilities as to what he was hiding was vast, and it included some pretty dark options. All of it seemed tiresome to Rose, and frightening. The longer she kept him in her thoughts, the harder it would be to avoid him. And the more likely it would be that she would encounter his darkness.

That day at the picnic, she and April watched him standing outside, right next to the porch, holding hands with his younger niece, the toddler, under a gray, foreboding sky. The clouds were moving in fast and low, building and billowing like waves, like a storm surge rushing in with a high tide. But it was still safely in the distance. So they watched. April and Rose watched, too, and April translated from Pennsylvania Dutch, though a translation was barely needed.

The little girl looked up at her uncle with wide eyes. And she pointed and said, "Rain."

"Yeah, li'l sprout," he said. "The rain is coming."

"Rain is coming," she said slowly, carefully trying out the phrase.

The girl let go of his hand, and she walked a few steps. And there was something striking and beautiful but also menacing about seeing her soft little body and messy ponytail out there under the churning gray sky. She looked back at her uncle. She pointed to the sky.

"The rain is coming," she said.

"Hold up your hands like this," he said and held both arms straight up over his head. He flattened both hands so the palms were facing the sky. "That way you can catch the rain in your hands."

The girl lifted her arms but had trouble getting her palms straight.

"Look at me," Micah said to her, showing her how to position her hands "Just like that."

She tried again and succeeded.

"Good job, li'l sprout!" he said. "You did it! Now you can catch the rain."

She beamed with pride and held her arms straight up, palms (mostly) facing the sky, catching some stray raindrops. Micah drifted out closer to her. And when he got close, she looked at him again and with a very serious air and the tone of someone delivering a very important piece of news, she said, "Look, rain!"

"Isn't it nice?" Micah said, and brushed her damp hair out of her eyes.

There was a sudden explosion of distant thunder. The child jumped, turned her head down, ran to him, and grabbed his leg. But then she let go and looked up again, out of curiosity, and took a step forward toward the storm.

"*Boom,*" she said, pointing to the sky.

"Big boom!" Micah said.

"Big boom," she repeated.

And after a pause, she said, "All done boom boom!"

She continued looking up at the sky. Finally she put her arms up, and said, "Up" and he scooped her up and kissed her cheek, and then he adjusted her onto his arm and fixed her ponytail, and the two of them, their eyes lined up right next to each other, continued watching that storm roll in, without a word. And when more thunder clapped, she would squeeze him and burrow into his arm. But then she would come out again, and they would continue watching.

As they watched the storm, Rose watched them. She watched every little tender gesture. And the more she looked, the more tenderness she saw in this man.

But that was then. Much had happened since then to complicate that picture in her mind. But the picture was still there. And so were the feelings. She just wanted to see Micah, his face. And to hear his voice. To know he was okay.

The days passed, and then the weeks. She even got antsy enough that she texted his lawyer, the public defender. And she almost immediately replied: *He's out!* Rose had been too proud to ask Joseph if he had seen Micah, but finally she gave in. Joseph told her that he'd been under strict orders from April not to bring Micah up, but, yes, he was out, and he was at home.

It had been more than two weeks since he'd walked free. And he hadn't made any effort to see Rose. The message was clear enough.

Rose threw herself into work for a bit. She was getting more interested in learning how to farm and was spending more time in the fields with Joseph and his siblings. One day, while she was in the fields, counting how many corn plants were silking, she saw a buggy pull up to the farm. Micah stepped out and looked around for a moment before heading toward the house. Without quite intending to, Rose threw down the paring knife she was using to examine the corn plants and tossed away the clipboard where she was keeping her records. She ran toward Micah. She ran as fast as she could to him, as though he would disappear forever if he made it into the house first.

He didn't see her running toward him until the last second. He turned around just in time for her to pounce on him and throw her arms around him.

"Oh, Micah," she said, right into his ear, "thank God you're free."

He looked at her in amazement, unsure what to say.

"I missed you so much," she said. "Can you ever forgive me?"

"Rose," he said. "I came here to apologize *to you*."

"For what?"

"For . . . not telling you how I really felt when you came to visit me."

"You didn't tell me *anything*, Micah," she said. "You didn't even tell me that you were really innocent! I asked, remember? I asked you straight out whether you committed that crime and you didn't deny it."

"They told me to watch what I said—"

"Who's 'they'?" Rose cut in.

"Whitey," Micah replied. "Well, not Whitey himself. But his guys. They're everywhere in the prison, you know? And they told me, very clearly, not to talk to you."

"Or else what?"

"Or else *you* would get in trouble. They would make sure of it. They told me the only way to save you from going to jail for a long time, or worse, was to just not say anything when you came around."

"Oh, Micah . . ." Rose said.

"It was the same way they forced me to help them with Caroline's body, and then to confess to killing her. They came to me, you know, just showed up one day. They must have been following me. They surrounded my buggy and forced me to stop. They told me what I had to do. They said if I refused or went to the police they would . . . I can't even say it."

"What? What did they tell you?" Rose said. "You can tell me."

"They said they would kill you."

"Oh, God, Micah, I'm so sorry you had to make that decision. I can't even imagine."

Rose leaned in close, took Micah's hand, and squeezed it tight.

Chapter Twenty-Three

Rose's bedroom door flew open. The light went on. It was April.

"Get up, babe," she said. "Up, up, up. We gotta go *now*."

April was throwing open Rose's drawers and stuffing clothes into a travel bag. She stopped for a quick second and looked at her sister, who was sitting up in bed, groggy and confused.

"Ugh, I'm sorry this happening. I'm sorry it's like this. I tried. We're gonna be fine, okay? But we need to go *right now*. We'll talk later."

She jogged over to Rose, pulled her up, and tossed some clothes onto the bed.

"Put these on," she said. "Grab only what you need. Solid shoes. Grab your phone and charger, your wallet. And let's *go*."

Downstairs, Joseph and Micah were loading supplies and food onto a flat-bed truck. April grabbed Rose's luggage, zipped it up, lugged it down the steps and directly outside, where Joseph heaved it onto the truck.

"We ready?" April said to Joseph.

"Yup," Joseph said. "Ready."

In the next moment they packed in to the truck. Micah, the only one of the four who had a driver's license, was at the wheel. With April sitting on Joseph's lap, they were just able to squeeze into the cab of the truck. Joseph rolled down the window and gave a signal toward the barn. Suddenly the horse and buggy took off toward the driveway and then the road. Rose, was who still waking up, watched this in wonder.

"What is going on here?" she asked, almost under her breath, and because they were packed in so tightly, almost directly into April's ear.

"Joseph's plan . . ." April said as the truck engine roared. "Whitey's guys are coming. Cops tipped us off."

"Who's driving the buggy?" Rose asked.

"A couple cops," April said. "But it's just a decoy. If anyone chases it down, they'll get a surprise."

Rose watched as the horse and buggy disappeared at the turn to the road.

"We're going the other direction. . . ." April said.

The truck rode over the lawn, toward the forest.

"What other direction?" Rose said, grabbing the passenger side door to steady herself during the bumpy ride over the field.

"Yeah," Joseph said. "Hold on tight. It's gonna get even more shaky."

"Where are we *going?*" Rose demanded. "We're just gonna drive this truck into the woods?"

"Joseph secretly made a path for the truck to pass through," April said. "For just for this reason. He camouflaged it and everything. It's like a little street, but right through the woods."

"When did you do that?" Rose said to Joseph.

"For a couple months now," he said.

The truck lurched as it entered the woods.

"Hold on tight. It's not a long road. But it is *very* bumpy."

It was just after dawn. The very first light was softening the black night sky. There was just enough illumination to see a few feet ahead. Joseph had covered the headlights with a transparent blue-toned decal, to shrink the beam in order to avoid detection from afar, even if it meant moving more slowly. Not that they would have been able to drive quickly. For a long forty-five minutes, they muscled and finessed their way along Joseph's path, sometimes backing up and lurching forward to climb over bumps or to avoid ditches and rocks. For parts of the journey, Joseph got out of the car to help direct Micah forward. Finally they approached the far edge of the woods, and the two-lane highway beyond it. That was their destination. Once they got there, they could speed to their real destination.

Joseph, who was already outside the truck, tapped on the driver's side window and indicated that Micah should roll down the window.

"Cut off the engine," he whispered. "Don't turn it on 'til I tell you."

Joseph pulled the transparent blue decals off the headlights. Then he stalked carefully toward the edge of the woods and the road beyond it. Even during daylight hours, this road was not very busy. Now it was almost desolate. One car would pass maybe every half hour.

Joseph crouched down and watched for a long moment. He didn't like the way it felt out there. But he saw nothing. It was time to go. And so he turned around to head back to the truck.

A single shot rang out. He fell facedown into the grass. His left calf burned. He could tell immediately that it wasn't as bad as it could have been. But the bleeding was heavy and needed to be stopped immediately. Unfortunately there was no time. The shooter was still out there. Joseph army-crawled back into the woods, then limped toward the truck. He ripped off his shirt and pressed it against the wound. He climbed up and in.

"Don't yell," he said as he climbed in, covered in blood. "I'm fine—don't make any noise!"

"Joe. *Omigod!*" April said, as he put his hand over her mouth. She'd jumped onto Rose's lap. Joseph slipped into the seat next to the door and sank into it.

"They shot me," he said. "The bullet only grazed me. But they're out there."

April grabbed the first-aid kit that was on the floor of the cab. With shaking hands she took it out, removed a tourniquet, and tied it just under Joseph's knee.

"We need to go," Joseph said weakly. He suddenly felt faint.

"No, Joe, we need to stop the bleeding," April said. "And then clean up the wound."

"No," he said. "No time. We need to go. Right now. They're out there. Go. They shot me from . . ." He thought for a second. "They shot me from the left. So get out to the road and go right. Keep the lights off. Go slow. When you get to the road, turn the lights on, then go as fast as you can."

"Maybe we should go back," Rose said.

"Too risky," Joseph said. "We don't know what's waiting for us there. It's more dangerous than this option."

"But we know that there's at least one guy with a gun on this side," April said. "And he's ready to use it. Maybe the way is all clear back at the house."

"If there's one shooter here, there's probably five over there," Joseph said, slowly and breathlessly. "Here, we have the road. And the escape route. We're so close to it. We turn back into the woods, we have two big barriers: the woods, which make us sitting ducks, and then whoever is at the house. I'm guessing a few of Whitey's men are there. They probably have the driveway and road blocked. But here, on this side, there may only be one or two guys. Until he calls in the others. This is our best option now. Just get to the road and make a run for it. They probably only saw me, not this truck. They won't be expecting a truck to come out of the woods. If we move fast, we could get ahead of them."

"Joe . . ." April said.

"I'm gonna be okay. Just keep pressing this—" He took April's hand, and pressed it against his balled-up shirt on top of the wound.

Micah started the engine. Right before he put the truck into drive and released the brake, he turned to Rose and said, "If I get hit, be ready to grab the wheel." As they began to roll toward the edge of the woods, April, with her free hand, reached over Joseph and closed the passenger door.

They emerged into the open, into the spot where Joseph had crouched, and where he'd been shot.

"Get down," he said. "Micah, stay low."

He pulled April down onto him, winced in pain, but continued pulling her down. As they reached the shoulder of the road, Micah put the car into a slow right turn. A shot rang out. Nothing was hit. Then another, which hit somewhere in back, possibly on the flat bed.

"Drive!" Joseph shouted through clenched teeth.

Micah stepped on the gas, flipped the lights on, and they were off. Another shot rang out. Nothing was hit. Micah looked into the rearview mirror. Nothing. Then two headlights suddenly appeared.

"I think they're coming after us," he said as calmly as he could muster. "We're not free yet."

Micah was doing ninety miles an hour. The road was straight but a bit hilly. Every time they went over the summit of a hill, they momentarily lost sight of the truck that was trailing them. Joseph knew these roads well and had built a plan around his knowledge of the countryside.

"Remember what we said, Micah. When you lose sight of them on one of these hills . . . we have a few chances coming up. Don't make the turn unless you are completely clear. . . ."

"Yeah, yeah, I remember. I practiced it," he said.

For the next minute, Micah gradually brought his speed down and watched his rearview mirror intently.

"Making me a little nervous to slow down . . . they're gaining on us . . ." he said almost to himself.

"Brake on the down slopes, when you lose sight of them . . . don't want them to see that brake light and get suspicious," Joseph said.

"You know a lot about cars, considering that you've never driven one. . . ." April said.

"I studied for this," he told her.

"Guys, I need quiet now, okay?" Micah said.

Nobody said a word. A few minutes later, with the car cruising at sixty, the headlights in the rearview mirror went out of sight, and a left turn presented itself. Micah started tapping the brake.

"Hold on everyone!" he said as he made the treacherous turn. And just as he did, he peeked in the rearview mirror. It was all black.

"*Got it,*" Micah said.

They were now on an unpaved country road.

"Pull over, kill the engine!" Joseph said.

In one rapid motion, Micah did both.

Micah let out a big sigh and collapsed on the wheel for a moment. Rose squeezed his arm.

"That was so good," she said.

Six seconds later they all watched as the truck rocketed by on the highway.

"I can't believe that worked," Micah said, throwing his head back and taking another big breath.

"Joe, we need to get you to a hospital," April said. "Right now."

"I'm okay," he said, and when she gave a him a look, he added, "I *am*. The bleeding has stopped. The bullet just grazed me."

"Grazed you?" April said. "Are you serious right now?"

"Let's get to this safe house first. I'll clean up there, and we'll see if I need to go in. Micah, let's wait another fifteen minutes, then start the engine. I'll tell you where to go."

"Do you think . . . they'll come back this way?" Rose said to Joseph.

"I doubt it," he said. "They'll probably figure that we made a run for the interstate, which is the next exit. But there's just too many options for where we might be. They won't even know where to start looking. They'll probably just give up."

"For now," Rose said.

"Exactly. *For now,*" Micah said. "Whitey never really gives up."

When they walked into the safe house, a mostly-constructed home that Josepth was builing for a cousin, April breathed a sigh of relief and led Joseph upstairs. In the bathroom, she set about cleaning his wound.

"See," he said, "it wasn't so bad. It looked worse than it was."

"But you would say that," April said.

"Maybe. But please trust me. I would tell you if I needed to go to the hospital."

"I know you would, babe," she said, as she finished wrapping the wound.

"I still can't believe they actually shot at you."

"I wasn't expecting that," he said. "And it makes me think that the police are right."

"Now you know I can't possibly ever agree with *that* sentiment."

"This whole time, ever since the trial, they've been saying that Whitey will try to stop Rose and Micah from working with the cops, and from testifying against him in the future."

"Maybe," April said, "but Rose thinks Whitey has other motives. She thinks he just wants to talk to her face-to-face."

"But that's what I mean," Joseph said. "If that's all he wanted, why are his guys coming out shooting first?"

April got very quiet.

"Look, I know you want to support her in everything," Joseph said. "But we need to be careful about allowing her to get close to him. These messages he sends her, about wanting to talk, it's just a trap. We need to be firm with her about this."

April didn't reply right away. Until finally she said, "You may be right."

Later, April fell into a deep sleep. Her anxiety kept her up for a bit, but her exhaustion won out in the end. Which was why she didn't hear her door open. But Joseph did. And he immediately shook her awake. Through the fog of sleep, she saw a figure standing in the door, brightly backlit. Even before she heard the voice, she could tell that it was Rose. Even so, she started. Something seemed off.

"Guys," Rose said weakly. "We need to go."

Her voice sounded so tired, and her manner was so odd and detached, that April was certain Rose was half-asleep. Maybe sleepwalking. She hardly sounded like herself. And the slowness of the speech also didn't match the urgency of the message.

"Hon," April said, "are you awake?"

"What?" Rose replied. "Obviously I'm awake. We're talking, aren't we?"

"I guess."

"Guys, I'm serious. We need go *right now*. He's coming here. He just told me."

"Oh, Rose," April said.

"It was a *dream,* Rose," Joseph said, with uncharacteristic impatience.

"No, it wasn't, Joe. I know what a dream is. I wasn't even asleep."

"Fine," he said, burying his head back into his pillow. "It's not a dream. But that doesn't mean it's really him either, does it?"

"Do you want to find out?"

"I'll risk it," Joseph said into his pillow.

"Don't you have a back-up place?" April said to Joseph. "You mentioned something like that to me."

Joseph sighed into his pillow. He sat up. And he looked at Rose.

"Did Whitey's message seem real?"

"Why do you think I'm waking you up?"

April grabbed Joseph's arm.

"She's right," April said. "Let's not waste any time here. Do we have a backup place?"

"Yes," Joseph said. "There's a place. It's not so easy to reach."

"Perfect," Rose said.

April ran downstairs when she heard the shouting.

"How did he know we were here!" Joseph was shouting at Micah.

Rose had never heard him raise his voice, and she shrank into the corner.

"Joe, I think we need to go. Let's talk this over later."

Joseph got into Micah's face.

"Did you tell him? You told him, didn't you!"

Joseph reached into his bag and pulled out a gun. He pointed it at Micah.

"Joe, no, what are you doing!" April said.

"Tell me right now, Micah," Joseph said, "Are you giving information to Whitey?"

"No, I swear," Micah said.

"Do you talk to him?"

"No, no, I don't. I have nothing to do with this. Please . . ."

"If I open up your bag and find a phone, can I check it?"

"I don't have a phone," Micah said, shaking. "You can check my bag."

"Okay, put the gun down right now," April said.

Joseph slowly lowered the gun.

"Lock it in the holster," April said. "And I'm holding on to it for now."

"I speak with him," Rose said. "I speak to Whitey. As you all know."

"You told him where we are?" Joseph said.

April shifted her body in front of Joseph.

"Back off, Joe," she said.

"It's okay, Ri," Rose said. "No, I didn't tell him where we are. But he knew. And I guess he could tell by my reaction when he mentioned it that his guess was right."

"How did he know?"

"He's been having you followed," she said. "He follows all of us. And he uses all of his connections to get more information. And then he pieces it together. Your secret path in the woods, the one for the truck? He knew about it. He had an idea you were up to something there. His guys were right there, waiting."

"They weren't *right* there," Joseph said.

"They were close," Rose replied.

"You need to stop talking to him," Joseph said.

And when April gave him a look, he added, "Don't look at me that way. We talked about this! We can't have her talking to Whitey anymore."

Now April gave Rose an apologetic look.

"What if talking to him isn't the problem?" Rose said. "What if it's the solution?"

"Is that why they shot me?" Joseph said. "Because they want to talk?"

"Whitey regrets that that happened."

"I can't believe this," Joseph said. "Are you going to tell him where we're going next, too?"

"No, of course not," Rose said. "I didn't tell him this time, either. He *knew,* Joseph. Are you listening to what I'm saying? He knew because you came here a few times, to prep the place. That's all it took. He figured out the rest."

"Fine," Joseph said. "He won't figure out where we're going. I haven't been up there in years. Haven't even talked about it in years. I built the place for a hunter, so that he could be out in the field. He died and left it to me. I've barely even thought about it. Unless Whitey can read *my* mind, too."

"Okay, that's enough," April said. "We need to go."

* * *

They threw their gear into the truck and piled in again. Joseph asked April for his gun back. "We don't know who's out there now, waiting for us again," he told her, and she reluctantly agreed. It was early morning now, but the roads were still almost completely empty. Joseph instructed Micah where to drive.

"Are we lost?" Micah said, after getting off an exit ramp for the third time and looping around to drive the opposite direction on the highway.

"No, we're not lost," Joseph said. "Just making sure nobody's following us."

After he felt confident that they were not being trailed, Joseph led them to a small grocery store off the side of the highway. Behind the store there was a large parking lot, much larger than what was needed for the small shop.

"I think there used to be a church here," Joseph said.

As per Joseph's direction, they parked near the shop, not too far away to draw attention.

"Here we go," Micah said as he put the truck in park. "We should be good to keep this here."

"We're staying at this grocery store?" April said.

"Nope," Joseph said. "Over there . . ."

Joseph pointed to the parking lot. They all looked for a moment.

"Over *where?*" Rose said.

"The . . . parking lot?" April said.

"Nope, keep looking . . . those woods after the parking lot. Now, look up . . . those woods go directly up. There's a big hill up behind there. That's where we're headed."

"We're hiking?" Rose said.

"Yup, we'll carry just what's necessary. Keep the rest down here in the truck."

"Is it far?" April said.

"It's farther than you'd want it to be. Least, that's how I remember it. Also, it's a climb."

"We're camping?" Micah asked.

"Nope," Joseph said. "Probably pretty rough up there. So, pretty much like camping, least until we can fix it up."

"Do you know how to get *up there?*"

"We'll find out, won't we?"

For almost two hours they trekked in the woods, sometimes on what appeared to be a path, sometimes not. At some points they needed to clamber up rocky terrain. Joseph had blazed the trail five years earlier, when he'd first built the hunter's lodge. Most of his trail marks were still visible. Some were not. Some had been blazed on trees that were no longer standing. They lost the trail a few times, and each time it felt as if they would never find it again. But they pressed on, too tired to complain. April wanted to complain but she saw how stoic Joseph was being, even with his limp, so she just pressed on quietly, and quietly helped him along, too.

At every step of the way, Joseph kept a constant vigil, to make sure nobody was tracking them. There had been only a single truck that passed by them on the road, and it hadn't stopped. Joseph also kept a suspicious eye on Micah.

"These guys might be following us, unseen in the woods," Joseph announced. "So make sure to listen carefully. too."

* * *

Just as Rose threw down her bag and said, "I don't think I can go on anymore," Joseph announced, "We're almost there. See," he said, pointing up the messy trail, "we're just a few minutes away." When they got up to the cottage, April's heart sank.

"You can't be serious," she said. "*This* is it?"

"Give it a shot," Joseph said. "It's nicer inside."

With a few tools that he'd brought up, he unhinged the door and removed it, and they walked in.

"It's cute!" Rose said, as she threw her bag down in the corner. "It's like a big treehouse!"

"It's in better shape than I expected," April said.

"I sealed it pretty good," Joseph said, inspecting it. "Some water damage here and there. But I can fix that later. Should probably put the door back on its hinges, or we could get some guests in here."

"Joe, thank you," Rose said.

"Before you thank me, you might want to see the out-house first," he said.

Chapter Twenty-Four

The next morning Rose woke up in Micah's arms. Since there was only one room in the cottage, and no beds or even couches—only a table and some chairs and benches—everyone slept on the floor, using their bags and clothes as makeshift pillows. Since neither Rose nor Micah was quite aware that they'd slipped into each other's arms, they both jumped when they woke in that position. Micah woke first, a few seconds before Rose, so he jumped first, waking up Rose, who jumped next. They both quickly rolled to their other sides, and that commotion woke up April and Joseph, deepening the awkwardness even more.

April, sensing what had happened, gave her sister a sly look. But Joseph didn't notice at all. He was already thinking about the next steps.

"How much food do we have?" he groggily asked the group. They began to unpack the food they had grabbed during their hasty departure. It was enough for two days.

"Okay, good. But we need to get moving," he said to

April. "We need to do some shopping and then get back here to make some repairs to this place."

"We?" April said.

"Me and you," he replied. "We need to hike back to the truck and run some errands. Then hike back up."

They gathered their things, and as they walked out the door, April looked over her shoulder and gave her sister a little wink. And then Micah and Rose were alone.

"I should probably start working on this place," Micah said.

"I can help you," Rose said.

Micah gave her a skeptical look.

"I can!" she said. "Just because I'm not, like, a master woodworker doesn't mean I can't do *anything*."

"I didn't say a thing!" he said.

"You didn't need to," Rose said. "You might be able to build things out of wood, but I can read *minds*. Remember that."

"What am I thinking right now?"

Rose looked at him for a long five seconds. She grinned, then he grinned. Then she laughed and shook her head.

"This is not how it works."

"How does it work?"

"The problem is that you're kidding around," she said, "but you can't do that. Or it doesn't work."

"I'm not kidding!" he said. "I really want to know."

"But you laughed! You can't laugh or it won't work."

"I didn't laugh!"

"You did! You totally did."

"Fine, but I laughed because *you* did. You laughed first!"

"Okay, fine," Rose said, "maybe I did."

"Thank you," he said. "Now, will you show me?"

"I'm not ready, *okay?*" Rose said with a sudden sincerity that surprised both of them.

"Oh, okay," Micah said. "I didn't mean to . . ."

"It's fine," she said. "I know you didn't mean anything. It's just, it's a serious thing."

"I know that," he said.

"Do you?" she asked. "Not trying to be mean about it . . . but *do* you know? I don't know what you know. I hardly know you at all."

"I think you do know things about me. I think you just don't want to admit it. You keep me away."

Rose turned these words in her mind for a moment.

"I can feel your pain sometimes. I see it. Your sadness. I can see that it follows you like a shadow. It's a presence."

"After I lost my sister, she came to me three times."

Rose didn't say anything. But she put a hand on Micah's shoulder and looked at him.

"I'm not talking about dreams. I dreamt about her all the time. Still do. I'm not counting those. I mean she *came* to me. In person. While I was awake. . . ."

"You don't need to explain," Rose said.

"She didn't speak," he said. "It happened during those first few months."

"People don't die right away," Rose said. "Their signal is strongest in the first year after their heart stops."

"I've never told anyone that," he said. "I don't want people to think I'm crazy."

"Is that what you're afraid of, Micah? Being seen as crazy?"

Micah thought for a moment.

"No," he said. "You're right. That's not really what I was afraid of. I was afraid that someone would convince me that . . . it wasn't true. They would convince me and I would believe it. I would believe that it was just my, I don't know, grief talking."

"You were afraid they'd take her away from you again, and this time for good. Was that it?"

Tears filled Micah's eyes.

"Yes," he said. "That's it. That's what it was. That's exactly what it was."

"Micah, I have something I need to tell you."

She took both of her hands and put them on his hand. He put his other hand on hers and squeezed them tight.

"Micah, what is your sister's name?"

"A-Annie," he said, choking up.

"Micah, look at me, sweetie."

Micah looked at her. She wiped away his tears.

"Micah, dear soul, Annie came to you. Okay? She did. She came to you three times. It was *her*. It was your sister. She came to you because she loves you. That's it. That's the explanation for it. And you know it's true because it happened to you."

"I know that. But it means a lot to me . . ." he said, breaking down. "It means a lot to me that you say it."

Micah cried in her arms—and Rose, too, felt like crying. Finally, Micah grew exhausted and then they lay down, holding each other in silence until they fell asleep.

* * *

They had gotten into a daily routine in the hunter's lodge and had been working so hard to figure out how to make it livable that they forgot, for a moment, that it wasn't really livable. And that it was temporary.

"What's the next step?" April said, as they all sat down for dinner, around the newly refurbished firepit. "We can't live like this forever. We can't just always be on the run."

"Should we check in with the cops?" Rose said.

"We know they can't really help," Micah said.

"Or won't help," April said.

"We should talk to them again, though," Joseph said. "We could use them."

"We need more information," Micah said. "They're never gonna find anything out themselves. We can use them as muscle. But to actually find out where Whitey is . . . we need to do that ourselves."

They all sat quietly for a moment, listening to the fire crackle, listening to the sounds of the woods.

"Why don't we grab one of Whitey's guys?" Joseph said. "Get him to talk to us. To the police."

"And how do we do that?" April said.

"We lure them out," Joseph said, "trap them."

"Sounds risky," April said.

"Sounds kind of crazy, actually," Rose said.

They all looked at Micah.

"I don't know," he said. "What are the other options?"

"I could . . . set up a meeting with Whitey," Rose said.

"Absolutely not," April said.

"Just to lure him out," she said. "So we can figure out where he is. And then we tell the cops."

"That's an idea," Joseph said.

April shot him a look.

"No," April said.

"Ri, I wouldn't even meet with him," Rose said. "I would just set up the meeting, and then, I don't know, the police could show up instead of me."

"Nope," April said. "He's not that dumb. And then he'll just be even angrier, and harder to find. He'd only really come out of hiding if he could be convinced that you'd actually meet him. And that's definitely not happening."

"Maybe we should ask the cops how they'd do it," Micah said. "Don't they do these kinds of things?"

"I'm not even sure the cops would go for that plan," April said. "They don't seem to want to move on him. Even if we did give them all the information. Even if we set up the whole thing. That thing about him being a protected FBI informant . . . I think it's real."

"It probably is. But I think we should go in and talk with them again. See if there is any willingness to help us. Because, in the end, this is simple: either they take Whitey out, or we do. And we would prefer that they do it. So that's where we should go first."

"I think you may be right," Rose said.

"We might still want to grab one of Whitey's guys, and get information out of him," Joseph said. "It would help to know more when we go to speak to the cops."

Joseph patted Micah on the back.

"He and I will do the heavy lifting," Joseph said.

"I don't like that plan," April said. "There's a lot of risk, and only a slim chance that it will actually get us what we need. Even if everything went as planned, and you didn't get shot and killed in the effort, chances are you'd get this guy and he'd know basically nothing. It's just not worth the risk."

"If you want information on Whitey," Rose said, "I'm the best bet."

"Rosie, no," April said.

"I am. I can talk directly to him. And nobody needs to get jumped and blindfolded, or whatever. Let's use my skills here."

"I dunno," April said. "I don't like that. I don't want you talking to that man."

"Ri, I understand, but we can think it through so that it's safe."

"But in the end," Joseph said, "if Rose does talk to him, the goal would still be to see him, to get him out into the open, in real life. . . ."

"I know. Exactly," April said. "And that's why I don't like it."

"What other choice do we have?" Rose said.

They all sat in silence for a bit.

"Okay," said Rose, "let's figure out how to do this."

The next morning, they heard some rustling outside. This was not uncommon. But it was always cause for some concern. Next to Whitey's men, hungry bears posed the biggest threat. And unlike Whitey's men, a bear attack could hardly be repelled with just a handgun.

Joseph peeked out the window to see what was moving outside. He immediately saw that it wasn't bears. It was a man, stalking through the woods with a rifle. He was wearing the bright orange gear of a hunter. Probably he was a hunter. Or he was one of Whitey's men, pretending to be a hunter. Whoever he was, he didn't seem to see the hunter's lodge, even though he was only feet away from it. Joseph ducked and put a finger over his lips so that the others would stop moving and talking. Then he crawled out to the deck of the hunter's lodge and pointed the gun directly at the man.

"Drop that rifle," he barked. "And put your hands up."

The man dropped the rifle and put his hands up. He looked around, slightly confused, until he spotted Joseph and saw the gun pointing at him.

"I dropped it!" he said. "Don't shoot!"

"Keep them up," Joseph said, holding his gun steady as he got to his feet. "I'm gonna ask you a few questions. You tell me the truth, and you'll be fine. And you'll get home tonight and have a beer, and everything will be great. You lie to me, and you'll never get out of these woods. Do you understand me?"

"Yes, yes! I'll tell you anything you want to know."

"Why are you walking around here with a rifle?"

"I'm hunting deer, sir. See, I'm wearing the gear—I can show you my hunting license." The man lowered his hand into his vest, and Joseph ducked, and shouted, "*Hands up where I can see them!*"

"Sorry, sorry! I have the license, if you want to see it."

"Who do you work for!" Joseph said.

"Oh, I work for myself. Got my own business, doing windows for houses and businesses."

"Do you know who Whitey is?"

The man didn't reply right away.

"Don't think I do," he said.

"How do you field dress a deer?" Joseph asked.

The man spelled out the first few steps, from the coring incision, up to removing the windpipe.

"Okay, fine, that's enough. Stay where you are!"

Joseph, keeping his gun trained on the man, yelled into the house for Micah. And gave him instructions.

"There's someone coming down there now," he told the man. "He's coming to get your ammo. All of it. Once he has it, you can have the rifle back. And then I want you out of here and don't want to see you again. You're not hunting here, understand?"

"Yes, sir," he said.

Micah went down to the man and collected all of his ammunition. He picked up the rifle and asked the man to give him instructions for getting the ammunition out of it, and then he took that, too. And when he was done, he handed the rifle back to the man.

"Now go," Joseph said.

That night, they sat around the fire and reflected on the incident.

"I shouldn't have asked him about Whitey," Joseph said. "I shouldn't have mentioned that name."

"Oh, that guy was *harmless,*" April said.

"Even if that's true," Joseph replied, "which I'm not so sure about, but even if he was harmless, he could run his mouth when he gets to town. He could mention Whitey. And if the wrong person overhears, we could have a problem. This guy knows exactly where we are. But that's the easygoing explanation. The other explanation is that this guy works for Whitey and knew exactly what he was doing here."

"What do you want to do about it?" April said.

"I think it's time to begin thinking of the next step, the next place we should go. And the next thing we should do."

"Or," said Rose, "we could just take Whitey on, face-to-face. Stop running."

No one replied, and they all listened to the sound of the fire sizzle and pop in the cool air.

Rose's conversations with Whitey were becoming more and more vivid. She would go out into the woods around dusk and find a quiet spot. And there she would close her eyes and commune with him. It was frightening how three-dimensional his presence was. One night as they spoke, she had to end the conversation almost as soon as it had begun. It was just too intense.

"He's close," she said, as she walked back into the lodge, following one of these conversations.

"He told you that?" Joseph said, taking a break from starting a fire.

"No," Rose replied. "He didn't actually say that. But I can tell. I can feel it."

"What does it mean that you feel it?" April asked.

Rose thought for a moment.

"It's not exactly like a signal, you know, like radio waves or whatever," she said, "but it's also not completely different from those. So, like, the signal, or whatever it is, can be weaker or stronger."

"And it's strong now?" Micah asked.

"Stronger than ever," she said. "Like almost too strong to take."

"And that means he's *closer,* nearby?" April asked.

"I think so. Honestly not sure," Rose said. "It means something, though. Maybe he's getting stronger? Or maybe, I dunno, our connection is getting stronger."

Rose caught Joseph and April exchanging a look.

"Whatever it is, though," Rose said, "I don't like it. I don't like how it feels while it's happening. Or what it means."

"Maybe you should ask him where he is," Joseph said.

"Isn't that a bit obvious?" April said. "Like do we think a fugitive on the FBI's Most Wanted list is just gonna be, 'Oh, I'll tell you exactly where I am'?"

"I can try to get him to talk about where he is," Rose said. "I think I could come up with a way to make it seem natural."

But she didn't need to do much to coax him to talk. Because the next time they spoke, he began by telling her that he had returned to his compound.

"I'm home, darling," he said to her. "Back in the Community. It's been so lovely to see everyone. Even though there's one empty chair at the table. Please come home. Won't you?"

"Aren't you afraid to go back there?" Rose said.

"Never," Whitey said.

"What about getting arrested?" she said.

"For what?" he said.

"For the long list of charges that . . ."

"I told you many times; the police will never arrest me. Because if I go on trial, I will reveal things about them. I will use the trial for that purpose alone. Not to vindicate myself but to indict them. And they know it. If they ever come for me, it will be to kill me."

"Isn't that worse than being arrested?"

"You know my teachings on this. I do not recognize death as real. The only real thing about death is the way it makes us fearful in our lives. That fear becomes real. But only if you believe in it. And I do not. It means nothing in my life."

"Do you think you will die because you returned?"

"None of these thoughts crossed my mind," he said. "I'm just so happy to be back. When will you come to see me?"

"I need to think about it," Rose said. "The last time I saw you, if you remember . . ."

"Of course I remember. We communed with my sister. Are you saying we didn't?"

Rose thought for a long minute.

"Are you still there?" Whitey said.

"Yes," Rose said.

"Did we not commune with my sister Hefsibah? Did you not merge with her?"

"Yes," Rose said. "We did commune with her. I can't deny it. She was there, just as you're here right now."

"Oh, Hefsibah! I knew you'd return to me. You always do."

"But I'm *not* her," Rose said. "I'm not. I'm Rose. I know I look like your sister. And my life crosses over with hers, maybe. And yes, it is weird that she comes back when I am around. But I almost died because of this communion. And I wasn't afraid of death! Remember? I stepped into the coffin willingly, and without any fear, just as you taught me. But I was deeply scarred by the experience."

"You wouldn't be scarred if you had stayed in that coffin."

"You know what? You're right. It wasn't about fear or about me being scarred. But it was still a terrible mistake. It would have been so wrong if I had died. It would have shattered the life of *my* sister. You say death isn't real. Well, that *is* real. My sister's experience of it would be real. I can't do that again."

"It will be different this time."

"You need to promise me that if I come to see you, I will return, alive and well, to my sister, as soon as the meeting is over."

"I can promise you whatever you want me to promise you."

"You need to promise it clearly," she said.

"I will agree to any conditions," Whitey said. "And you need to make me a promise, too. Promise that you will bring back Hefsibah for me."

"All I can do is try," she said.

"We both know you can do it," he said. "I want you to promise you will stay, and not get scared and leave."

"I can promise to think about it."

Chapter Twenty-Five

The next morning, they were awakened by the sounds of rustling in the woods. April woke up first and shuffled over to the window to see what was out there, thinking she would see some deer. When she saw what was actually out there, she immediately fell to her knees, so as not to be seen in the small window on the north side of the hunter's lodge. She peeked out and continued to watch. There were at least ten armed men. She couldn't tell if there were more. They didn't seem like hunters. They weren't wearing the bright orange hunting gear. And their guns were heavier than hunting rifles. There were a lot of them. Nothing about their demeanor indicated that they were interested in deer. They had assault rifles slung over their backs and were tracking slowly and deliberately through the woods.

"Joe, come here," April whispered loudly.

"Is it important?" he said rolling over.

"Bunch of guys in the woods," she said. "They've all got guns."

Joseph jumped up, grabbed his pistol, which he kept

on a shelf, and ran over to where April was crouched next to the window.

"Look," she said. "I don't think they see us up here."

"I don't think so, either," Joseph replied. "I hope they don't."

"What are they doing? It's like they're looking for something."

"They seem to be making a trail," he said.

They watched for a bit longer. And then Micah and Rose joined them.

"Omigod," Rose said. "Who are they?"

"No idea," April said.

"Well," Joseph said, "that's definitely what they're doing. They're making a trail. See, that guy's carving into the tree. And that guy's cutting up stuff with a machete. But I don't think they work for the forest service."

"I guess this means we've got to be more careful out there," Micah said. "Make sure no one's around when we take a walk in the woods."

"Might mean we need to leave here," April said. "I mean, who *are* these guys?"

"Whoever they are, they seem to want their own private path in the woods," Rose said.

"We could find out who they are," Joseph said, "by following that path to the end."

"Right," April said. "We could do that. But we're not going to."

For a few days after that, they were all hypervigilant, only venturing out in pairs. They watched carefully from the window, to make sure nobody was around, before going out of the cabin. But after almost a week, they eased up. And they let their guard back down.

* * *

One morning April and Joseph had slipped out early to make a shopping run. When Rose woke up, she looked next to her and saw nobody lying there. And for a moment, fear gripped her. She quickly sat up and looked around. And then she said, almost to herself, "Hey, guys, where are you?" and got no response. She went outside to the little porch of the lodge and found Micah sitting there.

"Hey, you all right?" he said to her.

"Yeah, just a bit spooked. Waking up and not seeing anyone around."

"Oh, I'm sorry about that," he said. He patted the spot next to him, "Why don't you come sit here? We can watch trees together."

They sat for what felt like an hour but was probably only fifteen minutes, listening to the sounds of the forest coming alive, and the morning shadows shifting.

"It's so incredibly peaceful here in the morning," Rose said.

"Isn't it?" Micah said. "Almost like there's nothing to worry about at all."

Rose laughed, and then Micah laughed, too.

"That actually wasn't supposed to be a joke."

Then they both laughed again.

"I've been thinking about what you said to me that day, when I told you about my sister visiting me after she died."

"That it was real?" Rose said. "That you need to trust yourself?"

"Well, yes, I have been thinking about that, too. But I mean what you said to me right before that."

"Remind me," Rose said.

"About . . . talking to someone who's not there. I asked you how that works. . . ."

"I remember," Rose said.

"That's actually how we started talking about my sister. You told me, sort of kidding, that you 'read minds.' And I asked, 'Okay, what am I thinking right now'?"

"And I'd said, 'That's not how it works.'"

"But I think you know that I wasn't kidding."

"I have begun to suspect that . . . yes," Rose said.

"I think you knew it even then, when we spoke," Micah said. "That's why we ended up talking about my sister. About her visiting me."

"Yeah, it's true, Micah," she said after a long pause. "I do think you get it. I wouldn't give you so much of my attention if I didn't think you got it."

They sat for a while, watching the sky get brighter, the birds bolder in their flights.

"Why are you smiling?" Rose said.

"I didn't realize I was smiling."

"Yeah, you're just sitting there with a big smile on your face. So, like, what's the deal?"

"I liked what you said. That you give me your attention because you think I get it."

"Don't get so excited about it, Micah," Rose said. "I could change my mind at any time."

"You could. But you won't."

"But I *could*. And I might."

"But you won't."

They sat again, not speaking, but listening to the forest and to the distant sound of the river.

"I think I am ready, though," Rose said. "Ready to tell you how I speak to people through my mind."

"Are you sure?" Micah said. "If you're not ready, we can wait until you are. Or if you never are, that's okay, too."

"No, I'm ready. I trust you. It's not about reading someone's mind," she said. "It's about communication. It can't be one-sided. Both people need to be doing it. Both sides need to agree to it, and to do the work to make it happen. I also believe that it can't work unless there's some kind of deep connection, somewhere, somehow, between the people. Most of the time it doesn't even work. I don't know for sure, but I think both people need to be doing it at the same time for it to work."

"Are you . . . actually talking? I mean, moving your lips? Is that a dumb question?"

"Don't worry, it's not a dumb question! You don't always move your lips, no. At first I did. Now I've learned more. And I don't have to. But the funny thing is . . . I had to think about it when you asked. Because it *feels* like I'm moving my lips. It just feels like normal talking, face-to-face. But it's not. If you were watching it from outside, you would just see me lying there, or sitting, with my eyes closed. It probably looks like I'm asleep or meditating or something."

"That is how it looks," Micah said.

Rose gave him a look.

"I think it is, at least," he said. "I've seen you out there, in the forest. And I was wondering what you were doing. I thought you were meditating. But now, I'm guessing, I was seeing you talk to Whitey. . . ."

"The truth is that it is kind of like meditating. You need to sit for a while and put your mind into a kind of trance and imagine talking to the person—it's not really a hard kind of thinking but a soft one. It's more like easing into, sliding down a big slippery mountain and that mountain is made up of thoughts about that person, and it's this really gentle but forceful free fall into a deep pool of this person, and then they kind of show up suddenly or they don't. It's a bit like falling asleep. . . ."

"Wow," Micah said. "And what happens when they don't show up?"

"Then you just kind of swim around for a bit until you wake up. I honestly couldn't tell you whether the whole thing takes five minutes or an hour. I keep meaning to look at a clock before I go down."

For a long moment they watched as two deer came running by, and then abruptly stopped, sensing the presence of others.

"They're so human, aren't they?" Micah said.

"Yes, but the part of the human that is mysterious and alien," Rose whispered, and Micah nodded.

They watched for a bit longer, until the deer seemed assured of their safety and began grazing near some bushes.

"Can I ask you a question about something you said before?"

"Of course. You don't always have to ask me if you can ask me something. Sometimes it seems like you're scared of me."

"Well, I am a little bit. If I'm being honest."

Rose laughed. And the deer became alarmed and ran off.

"I guess I can understand that," she said. "But anyway, what do you wanna ask?"

"You said that for the conversation to work, you need

to have a deep connection with the person. Do you feel a deep connection with . . . *Whitey?*"

Rose paused for moment and looked at Micah. His eyes were so big and open and inquisitive.

"I do," she said.

She kept her eyes squarely on him, to watch for his reaction. He seemed amazed but without judgment. It was a look of sheer curiosity. Her trust in him was not shaken. But she remained vigilant.

"What do you mean by that?" he asked. "I'm not questioning you, just trying to understand."

"I know," Rose said. "It's a very good question. And believe me, it's something I think about a lot. I'd be lying if I told you I knew for sure. What I said before, that it can't work unless there's some kind of deep connection, *somewhere somehow*, between the people . . . what I meant by that is that there's some part of me that feels connected to this guy. I'm not saying he and I are connected in every way. Or that I agree with him or support him or anything like that. But there's some thread in me that connects to his life. And that's the part that opens the communication. I guess there's something we both need to talk about, and to talk about with each other, and so we do. It's not like we're friends, or anything else. To be honest, I wish he would just disappear forever. I hate him. But there's, I don't know, some unfinished business there, too. I dunno. And the more I try to explain it, to put words to it, the less it makes sense even to me. . . ."

"I think you're doing a pretty good job explaining it," Micah said.

"Do you think it's messed up that I have a deep connection to this guy who's basically a monster?"

"He's not a monster, though," Micah said. "If he were a monster, there would be no questions about him. We would know everything there was to know. But I do have questions."

"Like what?"

"Well, I still don't understand why he went after me like that. Why did he try to ruin my life? And why did he kill Caroline? I am still in shock over that. She was such a unique . . ."

Micah became emotional.

"I know," Rose said. "I didn't even know her that well. But I got that about her. She was on a journey. She was a seeker."

"Yes," Micah said, turning his tear-filled eyes to hers. "That was Caroline. It was also why it didn't work out with us."

"Because she was a free spirit?" Rose asked

"No, I loved that about her," he said. "I mean, because she left the Amish community. That's what ended it for us. It was a step too far for me at the time. But when I think back on it, I just . . . I don't know. Sometimes I think I should have left with her. It's not easy to do that. I don't even know if that's what I would want. But I didn't even give it a serious thought. I didn't have the courage to even *think* about it. I didn't appreciate what I had. And now she's gone, *really* gone. Because of him. And it could be explained by saying, 'He's a monster.' I've thought that. But it doesn't work for me. It doesn't explain things."

"You're so right, Micah. Saying he's a monster is not a good enough explanation. But I want you to know something about this guy. What he did to you, and to Carly, which is so horrible that it's too hard to even think about, it's the kind of thing that you want to push out of your mind, or to just stamp it with 'monstrous' and then forget about it. . . . It is that horrible, but it's actually not mysterious at all. All of it was because of me, Micah. The cops think he's trying to kill me—and you, too—because we could testify against him. But what they don't realize and refuse to believe is that he doesn't care about arrest or trial. He lives in a different reality. He is trying to lure me out. Or to punish me. Somehow provoke me into a reaction that he can use to continue our connection. He's obsessed with me. Or with what I can do for him."

Micah looked at Rose in a way that clearly told her he wanted to ask something but was afraid to say the words.

"Go ahead," she said. "You can ask."

"What do you . . . do for him?"

"I bring back his sister, Micah. You know the story of his sister, right?"

"Yes."

"I bring her back to him. And I don't mean memory lane stuff here. I mean, I am the link, the key that opens the door that literally brings her back. He needs me for that reason. Or he thinks he does. That's why he's obsessed with me. It's not really me he's obsessed with. It's *her*. And that's why he went after you and Carly—or Caroline—too. To bring me back to him, through this twisted logic of his."

"But how does he know about . . . *us?* Not that there's even an 'us' to know about. . . ."

"Maybe he sees something that we haven't yet acknowledged," Rose said. She raised her eyebrows at him.

"Maybe," he said. "But I mean, how does he even know that we know each other. . . ."

"You need to understand something about him. He has all kinds of FBI connections. He literally works with them. But honestly, he's smarter than they are. And definitely more dedicated. He spies constantly. He collects a lot of information. But it's more than that. He knows how to put everything together. He's on a quest."

"I guess that's good to know," Micah said. "But I can't forgive him for what he did to you. And what he did to Caroline. It's just so . . . terrible. She had her whole life—"

Tears filled Micah's eyes.

"You still love her, don't you?" Rose said.

"Love her?" Micah said. "I guess so. I knew her so well. Knew what her hopes were. Her family and her friends. And I know how this has crushed them. Which was why it was such a nightmare when they thought I was the one who . . . killed her. Her death is just so sad and unnecessary."

"That's true," Rose said. "It is unnecessary. That's exactly it. But if you want to understand Whitey, you need to see that to him it does seem necessary. All of it does. And that's what is so scary about him. He's not careless. He's very intentional. That's what makes him far more dangerous than most criminals. But it also makes him more, I guess, predictable? Does that make sense?"

"I think I know what you mean."

"Like with Carly. Sorry, *Caroline*. I keep calling her Carly because that's how I knew her. . . ."

"It's fine," Micah said. "I like it."

"Okay, good. So, with Carly? Like I said, the logic is always the same. It's . . . how can he get me back into his life so that he can get his sister back into his life. But then he does something so extreme, so awful. If you look at what is behind it . . . it's desperation. He went so far this time because he senses that he's losing this battle."

"But what can we do with that information?"

"To be honest, I'm not sure," Rose said. "But it means two things. One, that he's feeling tired; he wants this to end. And that's a good thing. But it also means that he's more dangerous now than ever. He feels more ready to risk it all, more likely to do crazy things. What he did to Carly . . . it shows us what he's capable of."

"So what do you think we should do?"

"I don't know. I don't think we should do what the cops are doing. Try to corner him, so that they can grab him and throw him into handcuffs. It won't work. If he's cornered, he'll just act like a trapped animal and lash out. And that means one thing: he will kill more people. Carly came to me because she was in trouble. I failed her. . . ."

"No, you *didn't,*" Micah said. "It's not your fault."

"It's not my fault, true. But I did fail her. And I can't make that same mistake again. Or more people will die. He's not going to be arrested. He's already made that decision. We need to do this another way."

"What other way?"

"I don't know," Rose said. "But I have to do it myself."

"Why? No, you don't! We're here for you. Your sister and—"

"They can't help with this," she said. "It scares them too much. And I understand that. I would probably feel that way, too, if the roles were reversed. I can't ask them to help. So I need to do this alone."

"Okay," he said, "but you don't need to do this alone. I am here for you. I can help."

Micah took her hand in his hands.

"I'm not sure you can, Micah," she said. "But I do need to be able to trust you. Can I trust you?"

"Yes, yes, of course you can."

"Can I trust you *not* to tell my sister or Joseph anything about what I'm telling you, even if it sounds kind of dangerous?" she asked, looking him directly in the eye. "Even if you see or hear something that seems like something you should tell them. Even if you think I'm in danger, you need to stay quiet. Can you do that?"

He hesitated for moment.

"Micah, I need to trust you. And you need to trust me about this."

"Okay," he said, "I do. I trust you all the way, Rose. And you can trust me."

Chapter Twenty-Six

Just after dawn, they awoke to a steady wail of sirens. The first siren woke April and Rose, and they sat up. Then the second and third and fourth sirens sounded. And they exchanged a long, worried look.

"Are they near?" April asked. "I can't tell."

Rose didn't reply but listened some more.

"They're not . . . coming here, are they?" April said.

"No," Rose replied. "I know where they're going. It's not here. But it's close."

"How do you always know these things?" Joseph asked, rubbing the sleep out of his eyes and yawning.

"They're going to Whitey's compound."

"*What?*" April said.

"His compound is close to here?" Micah asked.

"Pretty close, yeah," Rose said. "Remember those guys that day? The guys with the guns who were making that trail? Those were Whitey's guys."

"You knew that and didn't say?" April said. In the distance, the sirens died out.

"I recognized one of them," Rose said. "But I wasn't sure. And I didn't want to cause any upset."

"So were those Whitey's guys . . . or you *aren't sure?*"
Joseph said.

"Joe, easy," April said.

"No, I'm sure," Rose said. "Because later I followed
that trail, the one they were making in the woods. And it
led directly to Whitey's place in the woods."

"Oh. My. God," April said. "You did that?"

"Yes," Rose said.

"And you're sure it was Whitey's compound?"

"Are you joking now?" Rose said. "I think I know what
that place looks like. I mean, I was pretty shocked. I had
no idea where it was. Or that we were so close to it.
Though it is a pretty long hike."

"But you're sure?"

"Yes, Joe, I'm *sure,*" Rose said, rolling her eyes.

April shot a look at Joseph.

"I'm only asking because . . . I also followed that trail.
But I didn't find anything."

"The place is pretty well hidden," Rose said. "You'd
have to know what to look for. And I do. It was definitely
his place."

"Omigod, the two of you," April said. "Sneaking around
like that. You guys could have gotten killed. You're lucky
they didn't see you snooping around."

"The guards probably did see us," Rose said. "Nothing
gets by them. And they definitely saw you, Joseph. If you
were just walking around there in the open."

"So what should we do?" Micah asked.

"Well, if the cops really are there, maybe it means
Whitey's about to take a trip to jail."

"I doubt it," Rose said. "I don't think they'll arrest him."

"Sounds like they're going to try," April said.

"What do you think we should do, Rose?" Micah said.

Rose shot a quick grin at Micah.

"I think you and I should take a walk," Rose said. "Down that trail, to where it ends. And see what Whitey is up to."

"Absolutely not," April said. "That's my final answer."

"Maybe it's time to consider a new place to stay," Joseph said.

"How about we go back home?" April said. "I'll bet Whitey is too busy right now to bother us there."

"Maybe true," Joseph said. "Or maybe he's desperate enough try something. I think we should still stay away from places he knows to look for us."

"I think we're okay here," Rose said. "It is close to him. Closer than I want to be. But it doesn't appear that he knows we're here. If he did, he'd probably already have come. I say we stay here for now. Now, about that walk . . ."

"Rosie, no," April said.

"Listen, Ri. I'm going. I either do it secretly, when nobody knows that I'm gone, or I do it with your help and support. Your call."

April and Joseph looked at Rose without a word.

"Good," Rose said. "And Micah, you're going with me."

They left almost immediately.

"We can be back by nightfall if we go now," Rose said, gathering up her things and throwing them into a bag, which she put in Micah's hands as they began to walk.

They went quietly, without saying a word for an hour.

"Hey," Micah said, pulling out a water bottle, "let's take a water break."

They drank in silence. Rose handed her bottle back to Micah and smiled.

"This is nice," she said.

And when Micah gave her a look, she laughed.

"I mean, okay," she said, "weird circumstances."

"You mean that we're on a secret mission to spy on a psychopath who's obsessed with you. . . ."

"Yeah, exactly," Rose said. "But other than that . . . this is nice."

"Yeah," he said, "this is pretty nice."

A minute of silence passed, and then the only sound was their footsteps on the forest floor, stepping on leaves and stones and breaking twigs.

"*What's* nice?" Rose said.

"What?" Micah replied.

"*What* is nice?" she said. "You were all"— and Rose made her voice deep, and did her best impression of Micah—"'yeah, this is pretty nice' . . . but *what* is? What were you talking about?"

"Is that how my voice sounds to you?" he asked.

"Not just to me! That's exactly how your voice sounds, period. But don't try to change the subject. I asked you a question."

"What was the question again?"

"Ugh. I asked you what you meant when you said in your superdude voice, 'Yeah, this is pretty nice.' What did that mean? Answer me! Quit stalling."

"You said it first! I was just agreeing with you. . . ."

"Right! You agreed to it. *What* were you agreeing with, though?"

"It, this, I mean, the walk that we're on is, like, nice, you know?"

"Wow. So glad I asked."

"I'm not good with trick questions."

"You're also not very good with simple, straight-forward questions."

Rose began walking again. Micah watched her walk away for a moment, then jogged to catch up to her.

"It's nice to be here, in the woods, alone," Micah said as they walked, "with you."

Rose stopped. She looked at Micah and tried to suppress a smile.

"Keep going," she said.

"Far from everyone else," Micah said. "But close . . . to you."

"Good," she said, and continued walking. And over her shoulder, added, "Was that so hard?"

Within half an hour, Rose grew more anxious.

"We're close," she whispered to him. "Keep a look out for anything here."

"Should we go slower, or maybe move off the path?"

"Nah," Rose said. "Don't go too fast or make too much noise. But let's look normal and not like we're creeping around. He could have cameras around here. Better to seem like random oblivious hikers than like people who are sneaking in."

Just as she said this, something caught her eye. She grabbed Micah's arm and gestured for him to stay quiet. They stood for a minute, listening. Footsteps, twigs breaking. But it was just a deer. And so they went on. They got to a shallow brook.

"This is it," Rose said in a whisper.

"It is?" Micah replied, also in a whisper. Rose nodded.

"Where . . ." Micah said.

"I'm not going to point," Rose said, "but look over there." She nodded in the direction of a rock formation on the side of a hill. "You go into that, like, cave thing, walk for a bit, and there's an underground opening that goes into a bunker. If you came in through the other side, which is actually on the far side of this hill, you'd see a more clearly visible building. This is kind of the back door. It's the opening they actually use, though."

"Wow, this place is pretty crazy," Micah said.

"You don't know the half of it."

Just then, two uniformed police officers appeared in the woods at the side of the hill.

"This is a closed police perimeter!" one of the officers yelled. Rose noticed that the other officer had dropped his hand, unlatched his holster, and slipped his hand onto his gun.

"Oh, we were just on a hike here," Rose shouted back. "Is there a problem?"

"I suggest you go that way," one of the cops said.

"Okay!" Rose said. "Thank you, Officer!"

"Let's peek around on the other side," she whispered to Micah.

When they reached the side of the hill, they could see a phalanx of police vehicles and various officers, local and state, and also some FBI, milling around. There were two sharpshooters perched on either side, one on a nearby rock and the other on a hill. There were two TV news vans, and one reporter doing a live report.

"Wow," Rose said. "They're out in full force. If they

were smart, they would have more men in the back, though."

"Wanna go tell them that?" Micah said. And when Rose fell into a thoughtful silence, he added, "I'm . . . *joking.*"

"Maybe I should go over there," Rose said.

"What if you run into one of the cops you know?"

"So? I wouldn't mind messing with them."

"Rose, I dunno . . ."

"To be honest, the reason I'd go down there is *that . . .*" Rose pointed to the news vans and added, "You want to go on TV with me?"

"Rose, I really don't think . . ."

"Whitey will be watching the news. I'm sure of it."

"And so you . . . *want* him to see you?"

"Kind of, yeah," Rose said. "He's doing this for me. I want to show him that I know that."

"Rose . . ."

"Listen, honey, remember when I said, 'I need you to trust me'?"

"Yes."

"Well, I need you to trust me," she said.

Rose stood for a moment, thinking. Then she shook her head.

"Forget it," she said, finally. "Let's get back."

They got back shortly before nightfall.

"Thank God you're back," April said when they walked in. She grabbed her sister and gave her a big hug. Rose collapsed onto one of the benches.

"How far did you guys hike today?"

"It felt like twenty miles or something," Rose said, stretching her legs.

"Worse coming back, too," Micah said. "All uphill."

"Well, we took a little trip today, too," April said. "Down to that diner by the road. We had them put on the news. They wanted to see it, too. It's everywhere."

"Yeah, we saw the news vans down at the compound," Rose said.

"I can't believe you were actually there," April said. "It looked pretty crazy on TV."

"What did it look like to you?" Joseph said.

"To me?" Rose said, "It looked like the cops don't realize how many doors there are to that place. They're all on one side of the building, the most obvious side. Makes me think . . . they don't know what they're doing."

"Did anyone see you?" April said.

"Some officers found us," Micah said, "coming up from the back, in the woods. . . ."

"We told them we were hikers," Rose said, and laughed. "And they bought it. Again, doesn't make me think they know what's up."

"Did the police seem nervous?" April said.

"Only a bit," Rose replied. "They did have sharp-shooters and all that. What did they say on the news?"

"They said it was unclear why a wanted fugitive would go back to his compound, where he was sure to be found," April said. "They said he must want to get caught."

"He won't get caught," Rose said.

"Isn't he already caught?" April said.

"Just watch," Rose said.

"They said it was unlike him to make this kind of miscalculation," Joseph said.

"It's not a miscalculation."

"There's something I don't understand," Micah said, "Why don't the police just go in there after him?"

"Oh, yes, that's the big thing they were talking about on the news!" April said. "He's holding hostages in there. So the cops can't just bust in. They're trying to negotiate with him, though."

"How's that going?" Rose said.

"They said the talks are secret and that 'no details are being released at this time,'" Joseph said.

"That's because there are no details to release," Rose said. "He's not actually negotiating with them."

"How are you so certain?" April said.

"The cops can't offer him anything he wants," Rose said. "He didn't return here so that he could surrender. He's back because he wants something. And he plans to get it."

Chapter Twenty-Seven

"How did you know I would be here?" Whitey said, taking off his sandals.

"Because you told me," Rose said.

"Did I?"

"Not directly," Rose said. "You said, *If you come, come early in the morning.* I figured you didn't want me knocking on the front door. So I figured you might be here. This is where . . . we last parted."

"I remember," he said.

He rolled up his loose linen pants and waded into the water.

"Years ago I built that tunnel," he said, waving toward an exposed hole in the ground, "all the way from the compound, thinking I would one day want to escape. Run far away from here. And here I am today, not going anywhere. Just using it to go back and forth, to get some fresh air, and take a dip. There was never anywhere for me to run to. This is it for me."

"Aren't you afraid they'll catch you here?" she said. "You're not that far from the compound."

"I never bet on cops," Whitey said. "They're not stupid,

necessarily. They simply lack ambition. And you know what? Now that I say it, I realize it's more than that. They lack the imagination behind ambition. They can't even imagine what it would be like to be ambitious. They can't imagine what an ambitious person might do in any situation. And if they can't understand ambition, how could they even begin to fathom genius?"

"Do you consider yourself a genius?" Rose asked.

"Doesn't matter," Whitey said, running his hands over the top of the water. "What difference does it make?"

"What is your ambition right now, at this moment?" Rose asked, sitting down on a log.

Whitey laughed, bent down, cupped some water in his hands, and splashed it over his face. Then he walked deeper into the brook, and bobbed his head in, shaking the water off his face and hair.

"Ah, that feels so refreshing," he said. "So cold and wonderful! Have you ever had a moment of intense feeling, even something small like that, dunking your head into fresh water, and thinking 'if a dead person could still desire things, they would probably pay anything to feel this, even for just a moment. And here we are, now, alive, and we can feel these things anytime we want.'"

"Yeah," Rose said. "I have had that thought. Often, actually. Life is precious."

She gave him a look that was intended to be reproachful.

"You're judging me, aren't you?" he said.

"And what difference would it make if I were?"

"There's a reason why we have this . . . special connection," Whitey said as he walked out of the brook, wrung the water out of his clothes, and sat on a log near Rose.

"What's the reason?" Rose asked.

"*Hefsibah*," he said. "She's important to both of us. And so we're important to each other."

Rose didn't reply.

"You don't need to say a word about it," Whitey said. "I know you know."

"It's true," she said. "It is something powerful. And we share it."

"I want to see her again, Rose. I need to."

"I know," Rose said. "I know it has been your hope this entire time."

"It's all I want," he said.

"I know that."

It was the reason she'd left Micah, April, and Joseph sleeping in the lodge. The reason she'd walked through the darkness to this place where, once before, she'd almost died. She was willing to risk death again now. It was her only chance to ever be free.

Whitey fell to his knees, and tears filled his eyes.

"Will you do this for me?" he said.

She didn't reply at first.

"I don't know if I can," she said.

"I'm begging you," he said. He reached down into a bag and pulled out a gun. He pointed it at Rose, his hand shaking.

"You have to do this for me," he said. "It's all I have."

"What about—" Rose turned around and waved at Whitey's compound.

"That's a world of lies," he said.

"Those people worship you," she said. "They would do anything for you. They . . . love you."

"That, over there, is nothing," he said. "It doesn't even exist. In a few minutes from now, a charge will go off. The entire place will burn."

Rose froze. She turned back to look at the hill where the compound was located. As always, there wasn't much to see.

"Are you serious now?"

"Of course I am."

"You can't . . . you can't *do* that!"

"Do *what?*"

"Kill all those people! You don't need to. . . ."

"They're not gonna die. There will be a big fire, but not where anyone is. A message will go out to the cops, telling them that I'm surrendering and that they should come in and save everyone. They will. They will all be celebrated as heroes. It'll be a great story. You'll see."

"And what about you?"

Whitey kept his gun pointed at Rose.

"Me? Oh, don't worry about me. The only thing you need to worry about right now is bringing Hefsibah to me. Please."

"I can't do it if you're pointing that at me," she said.

Whitey thought for a moment. Then he put the gun down and flipped the safety. And then he extended the gun, handle first, to Rose. He put it in her hand.

"Please," he said. "It's all I have. Nothing else matters."

Rose looked down at the gun in her hand, at the safety latch, at the trigger. It felt heavier than it had looked.

"Okay," she said. "I'll do it."

Rose stood up, then sat down on the ground between the log and the river's edge. She cleared some twigs and rocks and smoothed the dirt with her hand. Then she lay down there and closed her eyes.

"*Hefsibah*," Whitey whispered. "Is it you?"

"I am here," she said.

"Show me that it's really you," he said.

"Remember when we used to make blueberry pie with Mamm? Just you and me and her, and we ate it hot out of the oven, right out of the pan. . . ."

She opened her eyes and looked at him. His legs seemed to melt and he collapsed onto her, crying. His body heaving in sobs.

"Oh, *Hefsi*. Oh, I miss you so much. Why are you always so far from me? Stay with me! How can I make you stay with me?"

But suddenly Rose was back. Even as Whitey continued to cry, she tried to bring back Hefsibah, but the signal was weak. It came and went. Rose took a deep breath and tried to concentrate. With each passing moment, Hefsibah seemed to be slipping farther away, returning for shorter and shorter moments.

"Oh, Hefsi," Whitey said, bringing her up to a seated position and putting his arm around her. "I need to be closer to you. I need to be able to see you more. How, though?"

"It won't be easy," she said, and at that exact moment

Rose felt Hefsibah slip away from her once again. Leaving her to herself, as Rose.

"Listen," she said. "I'm losing her. I'm speaking to you now as Rose, okay? I'm losing the signal here. It's . . . weak. Weaker than it used to be."

Whitey held her tight.

"No!" he said. "You can't let that happen. Please, keep her here."

"I'm trying," Rose said. "I really am."

Suddenly there was the small, low rumble of an explosion. And then a lot of smoke Rose shot up.

"The woods," she said. "We need to go. The woods will catch fire."

"They won't," Whitey said. "I designed this explosion to work. And they'll put out the fire soon. The compound will be destroyed. But everyone will get out."

"Should we . . . go?"

"We're not going anywhere," Whitey said. The sound of wailing fire trucks filled the forest.

"Please," Whitey went on. "Just give me a few more minutes with her."

Rose suddenly realized the gun was still in her hand. She'd been holding it the whole time. She squeezed the handle, took a deep breath, and closed her eyes. Hefsibah came.

"Gabey boy," she whispered.

Whitey squeezed her hand, the one without the gun in it. The smell of smoke reached them. The fire trucks had arrived at the site of the fire.

"I'm here, I'm here."

"Gabey boy," she said. And then her eyes suddenly

opened wide. She turned to him. She looked deeply at him. His mouth dropped.

"It's you! It's *you*. I can really see you!" he said.

"I see you, too," she said.

"Gabey boy," she said. She looked him squarely in the eyes.

"Gabey boy . . . come to me. Come."

"I'm here! I'm right here."

"No," she said. "Not like this." She was fading out again.

"I want to go to you."

"You need to do more than want."

"Tell me what to do," he said.

But Hefsibah was fading, and Rose was dazed. And mute. It was as if her lips were paralyzed. The smoke was getting thicker in the trees. Whitey slipped the gun out of her loose grip. She barely even noticed it leave her hand. Until the weight of it was suddenly gone. And until she saw it in his hands. He unlatched the safety and pointed it at her.

"Please," he said. "Don't do this. I'm running out of time. Speak. Don't make me do this. Speak."

But Hefsibah was gone from Rose. And Rose could not speak.

"I'll do it," he said. "You know I will. Don't abandon me now."

Rose closed her eyes.

"Gabey boy," Rose said slowly.

Whitey did not reply. Rose opened her eyes. She saw the tears in his eyes. She saw the gun he held firmly pointed at her heart.

"Gabey boy, come to me," she said, nodding gently. She took his hand, the one that was not holding the gun. "Come to me. Stay with me. Forever, Gabey boy. It's time."

When the smoke had reached Micah in the woods, he knew he was too late. He'd been following Rose ever since she'd slipped out of the cabin hours ago, moving a little distance behind her on the trail. But now he broke into a trot. And then, as the smoke kept coming, he began to run. He arrived at the ridge, right before the trail began to dip into the creek. That's when he heard it. A single shot. Unmistakably a gunshot. He continued running, now downhill, and slightly out of control, tripping on logs, and slipping over rocks on the incline. Finally he reached the creek.

He saw Rose, lying on the ground next to the water, blood pooling around her, pouring into the brook.

"No!" he shouted. "No, no, no, no. . . ."

He ran as fast as he could toward her.

"Don't go," he shouted. "Stay with me! *Stay!*"

When he reached her, she turned to him, her eyes streaming with tears, her face unscathed. He pulled her up.

"You're . . . okay?" he said, his eyes filling with tears.

Now he saw it. Whitey was flat on his back, his neck completely shredded and bloodied. The gun was still in his right hand, and his left was in Rose's hand. She was gripping it as though holding him for dear life. She was staring straight ahead, unblinking.

"He sh-sh . . . he shot . . ."

"It's okay, it's okay," Micah said, enveloping her in his arms and pulling her away from Whitey. "I understand! I understand everything. You don't need to say a word. It's over, Rosie. It's over. You're alive! Thank God, you're alive."

Chapter Twenty-Eight

The restaurant opening, long postponed, could not have been better timed. When the stylish sign for April's new restaurant, The April Rose, was unveiled, a *woo-hoo* went up from the large crowd.

"Who *are* all these people?" Rose said to Joseph, as they stood behind April while she pulled the veil off the sign.

"I have no idea," Joseph said.

If there was ever a modish crowd in Lancaster, Pennsylvania, this was it. Among the crowd of locals and tourists were food writers from Philadelphia and New York and Pittsburgh. Carmen, April's mentor from Philly, had hired a publicist whose constant calls and emails and caffeinated late-night texts had apparently worked their magic. The opening was truly an event.

For most of the celebration, April walked around the restaurant, chatting with guests and introducing people to each other. All the while, she was holding Rose's hand. In between two of these meet-and-greets, April leaned close to her sister and hugged her for a whole minute.

"Can you believe this?" April said.

"You're amazing," Rose replied. "You made this happen."

"This reporter wants to do a story about how I came *up from the mean streets of Philly*."

"If only they knew what that actually meant," Rose said.

"Exactly! I started to tell her some stories and she looked too horrified to continue the interview."

"Too real," Rose said. "They're not ready for it."

"You're the only one who will ever really understand all this."

"The April Rose . . . forever."

April squeezed her sister's hand.

"Okay, enough of that," Rose said. "Go out there and do the hustle."

At various points during the opening, Rose watched Micah from afar. She had seen him at some family picnics and other gatherings. But she'd never quite seen him in a social setting in her world, at a crowded opening like this. She watched him with curiosity, and she was not disappointed. Once, she caught him pinned up against a wall, as though by centrifugal force, surrounded by stylish ladies who were downing flutes of champagne. He held his champagne as though it were a grenade whose pin had been pulled. From across the space, he looked at her, with fear in his widening eyes, in an apparent effort to enlist her help. She mouthed to him, *Talk to people*. But he just shook his head and burrowed farther into the wall.

At another point, she caught him on his hands and knees next to the big railing, making some adjustments to some of the wall fasteners. She watched him for some time as partygoers stepped over him while he labored. Finally, when he was satisfied, he stood up, dusted himself off, and saw, almost immediately, that he was being watched. Rose was giving him a look that clearly communicated *What are you* doing, dummy? *This is a party.* But he just shrugged.

She was tempted to go to him, to lean on him, to stay with him. But she was also looking forward to doing that at the end of the party. To finding him after this was all done, cutting through the crowd to get to him, and, finally, collapsing onto him, and going home with him, falling asleep with him in the buggy, and processing all of it tomorrow at breakfast. She liked that he was her destination after this chaotic party. She liked that they were apart so that they could be even more together when it was all done. And she liked watching him from afar, seeing him struggle a bit without her.

She had been instinctively avoiding the restaurant's nearly wall-sized mirror. But in the bustle of the moment, she suddenly found herself right in front of it. She realized immediately why she'd been avoiding it. As one of the restaurant's investors, who was pursued by a strong aroma of perfume and wine, chatted with drunken merriment into her ear, Rose noticed a familiar face in the mirror. Carly. A shiver gripped Rose's hands and she almost dropped her drink.

As always with Carly's appearances, the feeling wasn't fear but a kind of sadness, of regret, of a distance growing more distant. But then Carly smiled. And it was not Carly's smile at all. It also wasn't Carly's face anymore. It was Whitey, smiling his ravenous smile, turning on his chameleon charm. Rose turned away. She excused herself.

Through the tangle of bodies and clinking glasses, she located Micah, talking to one of the other workmen, and she beelined to him and wrapped her arms around him from behind.

"He's here," she whispered into his ear.

"Who?" Micah said, smiling, not registering her tone.

"Him. Whitey," she said. "He's here."

"*What*?" Micah said, breaking her grip and turning around in alarm.

Rose took Micah's hands into hers and held each tightly. She caught Micah's darting eyes and brought his gaze back to hers. They were face-to-face.

"It's okay, Micah," she said. "Remember, they don't die right away. But he can't harm us anymore. Unless we let him."

"And we're not gonna let him," Micah said.

"Will you stay with me?"

"Rosie, I will always be with you."

In later times, when she thought back on that event, she couldn't remember anything else that happened. She couldn't remember anything else that was said. Couldn't remember meeting anyone else. All she could remember was climbing into the buggy with Micah at the end of the night, nestling into him as the buggy took off, and drifting off in the warm safety of his arm. She would sleep soundly that night for the first time in a very long time.

Please read on for an excerpt from April's story,

SEARCHING FOR ROSE

Courageous and vulnerable, April has survived Philadelphia's tough city streets. But when her sister disappears, April's search will lead her to the Pennsylvania Amish countryside— where the peaceful setting belies a brand of danger all its own . . .

With a childhood shattered by alcoholism and abandonment, April learned the hard way to trust only herself and her younger sister, Rose. But suddenly, Rose is gone without a word—and April's purpose in life is to find her. She has only one ally: Joseph Young, a handsome Amish man with whom she's struck up an unlikely flirtation in the bakery where she works. He's knowledgeable, steadfast—and when they join forces, April's life takes a radical turn . . .

In the heart of Amish farm country, April and Joseph grow closer. Yet April fears there's no future for them. Especially when vicious, too-personal warnings and strange attacks make her wonder just whom Joseph is really trying to protect. And as her unconventional investigation roils a community with much to conceal, April will find some secrets are killer—and some dreams may be too lethal to trust . . .

Chapter One

April wasn't the type to call the cops. She took care of her own business, didn't need to rely on anyone. That, at least, was the story she liked to tell about herself. But here she was, standing at the bustling center of Reading Terminal Market in downtown Philadelphia, talking openly with two uniformed officers as a small crowd of curious onlookers gathered around.

She was trying to explain, for the hundredth time, what had happened: her sister, Rose, was gone.

"What do you mean 'gone'?" one of the cops asked.

"Gone," April replied, already regretting this conversation. "As in disappeared."

Nobody had heard from Rose in about two weeks. She hadn't shown up to her job at Walgreens. She had, by all appearances, vanished into thin air. Wasn't it difficult enough for April to deal with this emotionally? Why did she have to explain it, too?

And there were things April wasn't saying. Things she'd barely admit to herself, much less tell the police. But here's what she did reveal: her sister's last words to

her, before she disappeared. I'm going to Reading. I'm
going to that bakery. Well, April was now at Reading Terminal Market, at that bakery, doing her part. She was talking to the cops, trying to make them understand.

"So you met her here?" another of the officers asked.

"No," April said, with a big sigh. "I didn't meet her
here. But she said she was coming here. That was the last
thing she told me."

"So you don't know if she actually came here that
day?"

"No," April replied, grimly.

A heavy wave of hopelessness suddenly overwhelmed
her. Her patience with the cops' questions was beginning
to wear thin, revealing the truer emotion underneath it. It
was the feeling she had been trying, for weeks now, to
avoid: raw despair. That was the exact moment she heard
a voice from inside the small crowd of onlookers.

"I saw her," the voice said.

It was a man's voice. April and the police officers, and
a few stragglers standing around in front of Metropolitan
Bakery, suddenly turned around to see who'd spoken.
Before April spotted the man, she saw the faces of the
people who had seen him: the looks were of startled surprise, curiosity, even amusement. And then she saw what
they saw. A young Amish man, with wide shoulders and
long limbs, stepped confidently forward. April had seen
him before, around the market, but never up close.

"Yes," he said, pointing to the photo that one of the
officers was holding in his hand. "Her," he continued. "I
remember seeing her. I saw her last week."

For a moment, nobody, not even the police, said a

word, as though waiting to hear what else the man might have to say. But, for the moment, he said nothing more.

The cops eyed him warily, skeptically.

"You sure?" one of the officers said.

"Yes," the Amish man replied. "I am certain."

And he really did seem certain. As he answered the officers' questions, April watched him closely. When they asked his name, he turned to April, as though addressing her, looked deeply at her, and said, "Joseph. Joseph Young." He pronounced his own name as though he were delivering a piece of dramatic news. To April, that's exactly how it felt.

His demeanor was unlike anything she'd ever seen in a man. Especially in one her own age. He seemed entirely in control, but without the need to assert his control over the situation. He held immense power in his large body but didn't bother wielding it, didn't seem to feel the need to show off. He seemed even more powerful for his restraint, more charismatic for his ability to master his charisma. To the police, he delivered strong, clear answers that were direct and sincere. He answered with a crisp "yes," never "yeah" or "yup." He wasn't trying to conceal something or compensate for anything. He was, in short, perfectly comfortable in his skin.

And what a skin it was. This man was head-turningly handsome. His serious face allowed for a quick smile, and April noticed he had dimples.

April was noticing, too, that she wasn't the only one seeing this. The eyes of the cops, and everyone who lingered in front of the bakery, were glued to this strange, beautiful man. Nobody wanted to interrupt him or let him go. Unless it was her imagination, it seemed that the cops were now only asking him questions as an excuse to keep him in front of their eyes.

And then there was his gaze. At various moments, he looked directly at April with intense green eyes—but why was he so interested in her? Maybe it was because she was the sister of the missing girl. Or was it because April herself was staring at him? Could it be because he was as taken with her as she was with him? Whatever the reason, the effect of that gaze on April was immediate, and it registered bodily. It felt as if she was standing in the hot beam of a theater spotlight. It was the same sensation she'd felt when she used to act in school plays. And, just as his eyes warmed her skin like hot stage lights, she felt the need to perform, to make a speech, to undertake some grand gesture—and increasingly the gesture she wanted to make was a dramatic exit. The heat was too much. She needed to do something, anything, not to seem like a deer caught in the headlights.

But the more April watched him, and the more she detected how intensely controlled he was, the more she also sensed that he was, just maybe, a bit too controlled. He would be hard to reach. A fortress. An impressive fortress, no doubt. But a fortress.

So mesmerized was April by this man that she hardly noticed that the police had stopped talking to him and had turned back to her, with some additional questions. She tried her best to focus on what she was being asked. But, in doing so, she lost track of the beautiful man. And before she knew it, when she looked around, he was nowhere to be seen.

* * *

That was the first time April paid close attention to the mysterious Joseph Young. But it wasn't the first time he'd studied her. In fact, he'd had his eye on her from the moment she'd made a dramatic entrance at the bakery in Reading Terminal Market almost a week earlier.

Joseph had witnessed the whole scene that day. From his own corner of Reading Terminal Market, at the Amish-run diner next to the bakery, he'd watched it unfold. That day, a Friday, he could tell that something was very wrong even before he knew what it was. He sensed trouble. And he wasn't the only one. The bakery's owner, Carmen, also sensed it.

Standing at her shop counter, carefully arranging the day's assorted delicacies—brioches and tartes Tatin, fresh out of the oven—Carmen sensed a commotion outside the bakery, somewhere out in the sprawling mass of Reading Terminal Market, which was packed with crowds shopping for a summer weekend. Carmen and Joseph, both, detected it as a minor disturbance of air, like the early breezes of an impending storm.

Just as Carmen rose to her tiptoes to peer over the crowd and investigate the situation, April lunged out of the mass of people, elbowing her way forward—seeming, as Carmen would later remember it, as though she weren't walking but somehow spinning, like a drunk ballerina pirouetting wildly. April sped headlong through the doorway of Carmen's bakery, tripped over one of the café chairs, and braced her body against the counter. Joseph, who happened to be standing nearby, saw this and followed her into the shop, where he witnessed the whole exchange.

"I need your phone," April had said, staring directly at Carmen. "I gotta make a call."

April was not blinking.

Carmen drew a long, loud breath through her nose.

"Sorry, hon," she said, straightening her back. "Can't do that."

Carmen wasn't from Philadelphia. But she'd lived there long enough, almost twenty years now, that she'd seen all of the mischief and misery the city had to offer. Half of the city, it seemed, needed her phone, or something of hers, at some point. Did a day go by when someone on the street didn't try to hustle her out of something?

Carmen quickly sized up the young woman standing in front of her. To survive in the city, a pretty girl like this would have to project an aura of danger. High and tight ponytail, hoop earrings, fire engine red lipstick to contrast with straight black hair and green eyes, high-waisted slightly baggy jeans, ripped at the knees and dotted with flecks of paint, red Air Jordans on her feet, a short, purple-black faux leather jacket, and a grimy fraying gray T-shirt. Philly was full of young women like her, Carmen thought. They're tough, sure, but mostly they want you to think they're tough. In other words: they're hiding something. Carmen tried to remain unmoved.

What gave her pause was the look on the young woman's face, the same look that had brought Joseph into the shop behind her: it was a look of genuine distress.

A memory flashed in Carmen's mind. Childhood. The farm. That girl.

Carmen came from country folk, who only went to hospitals if they needed surgery. Otherwise they used their own home remedies. Once, when she was really young, maybe eight or nine, she'd seen the most awful thing. Without any warning or previous sign of illness, a teenaged neighbor girl dropped dead one day while doing her chores in the dairy. Within days, the family buried the poor girl in the family plot. There was only one problem: she wasn't dead.

She'd fallen prey to a rare form of catatonia, which closely mimicked signs of death. When they'd checked for a heartbeat, they didn't hear it because the beats were so faint and so infrequent that her heart truly might not have been beating during the moments when they listened. She was, to all appearances, dead. And so they buried her.

The girl's younger brother, however, was so distraught at her loss that he'd spent all of his free time at her graveside, refusing to believe that she was gone. Incredibly, he heard clawing sounds from her tomb, and set out desperately to dig her out. In the end, they rescued her. But she was never the same.

Carmen had seen the girl after she'd been unburied. She remembered seeing her walk around town, at the market, so skinny, and with this doomed look on her face. Could the girl speak? She must have spoken. But Carmen never once heard her say even a single word. A ghost of a ghost.

She rarely thought about the unburied girl from her childhood. But that girl, her face, came to Carmen suddenly when she saw this stranger—the look in her eyes—

as she leaned against the bakery counter. The memory came with a startlingly vivid flash.

"Phone," April was saying, almost panting. "Please."

Carmen felt her defenses weakening.

"What's the matter, sweetheart?"

"My sister, she's . . ." said the girl, in an odd, absent sort of way, "gone."

Carmen retreated into the back to find her phone. As she rummaged through her purse, she saw April standing at the bakery counter, eating the bread samples, ravenously, until the plate was empty.

Why me? Carmen thought, then felt a bit guilty.

When Carmen returned to the counter, April was in tears. She was holding a photo of her missing sister, printed on a piece of office paper.

"This is the most recent one I got," she said. "Have you seen her? Her name is Rose. She comes around here a lot."

"Here?"

"Here," April said, "to this bakery."

"Oh," said Carmen, feeling a sudden knot in her throat. "I see."

She examined the photo. The missing girl had boy-short, bright red hair and big, mischievous eyes. She appeared to be a bit younger and a bit more punk than April. In the picture she was shown in a booth at a Chili's, intentionally leaning in front of another girl, impishly blocking her out of the photo. Her mouth was slightly open.

"What was she saying?" Carmen suddenly asked.

"Saying?" said April.

"Yeah," Carmen replied, handing the photo back to April. "In the picture. It looks like she's saying something."

April looked at the photo and smiled a tiny bit. "Probably something dumb."

"Well, she does look familiar, I think. That red hair," Carmen said. "But I can't remember when I might have seen her last. Not this week, I don't think."

Carmen handed her phone to April. She wiped her hands on her jeans, pulled out a piece of paper with a number on it, and began furiously dialing.

"I'm calling her friend," she said to Carmen. And then, a moment later: "Ugh." There was no answer. She left a breathless message.

Uh, hey, it's me . . . I'm calling from someone's phone because mine got cut off. Look, Rose's gone. I don't know where she is. I haven't heard from her for more than three days. You know she's not like that. I'm really scared. I don't need to tell you what I'm afraid of. I know you know. I'm at Reading now. Please call me back at this number or come here as soon as you can. I'm at . . .

She turned to Carmen.

"Metropolitan Bakery," Carmen said.

The Metropolitan Bakery, April said into the phone. Reading Terminal Market.

April put the phone back on the counter and looked helplessly at Carmen.

"I think you should call the police, hon," Carmen said.

"No," April replied with a vehemence that startled Carmen.

"I just think . . ."

"I'm not calling the police."

"Okay, hon," Carmen said. "Just keep it in mind, okay?"

For the next few hours April waited in the bakery, sitting at the table next to the door, staring out into the marketplace. Carmen made her a sandwich, which the girl at first ignored and then, in four rapid bites, devoured. At noon, when the bakery got crowded, a young woman about April's age approached her table and, seeing that she'd finished her meal, asked if April was about to leave. With teeth clenched in rage, April said loudly, "How about you keep walking." Carmen overheard this, sighed, dropped a croissant on a plate, walked briskly over to April's table, and slid the croissant in front of her.

"You will not talk to my customers like that," she said. "I'm running a business here."

April glared at her.

"Do you understand? Answer me."

"Yeah," April said. "I got it."

Even as Carmen handled long lines of customers, she'd turn an eye toward April. For hours, the girl sat in the same spot, almost motionless, just staring. Occasionally, she would stand up, look intently out the window, as though recognizing someone, and begin to walk toward the door, only to discover that it wasn't the person she thought, and then retreat back to her seat.

Joseph Young had watched all of this from afar. Whenever possible, he'd drift over toward the bakery, to see what was happening with the girl whose sister was missing. He considered going up to her and saying something. But what? And anyway, she seemed agitated, and not in the mood for company. Joseph decided to let her be—for now. But he was keeping an eye on her.

By the end of the day, April was still sitting there. As Carmen began to mop the floor, April suddenly jumped up.

"I gotta go," she said and made for the door.

"Wait!" Carmen called out. "What if your friend calls me back?"

"She's not my friend," April said over her shoulder.

And then she was gone, swallowed up in the crowded market. On her way out, she'd walked right past Joseph, who had drifted back toward the door of the bakery—possibly for the twentieth time that day—to keep watch over April. In her haste, she had bumped into him, and the contact had jolted him far more than he expected. The aroma of her perfume had reached him quickly and lingered powerfully for a moment before thinning out into the ether. Its fragrance was unmistakable. As Joseph watched April disappear, he named it aloud, letting the word pass over his lips like a gently felt secret.

Roses, he whispered.

Joseph had been so antsy to see April that he barely slept. But April did not show up at all the next morning, or during lunch. By 3:00 p.m. Joseph was losing hope. By 5:00 p.m., he was fairly certain he'd never see her again.

Carmen, too, was preoccupied with thoughts of this troubled young stranger. On her postwork walk home,

Carmen kept her eyes wide open, looking for April's missing sister—but she was also looking for April herself. The search went on for two days. During this time, Carmen called and re-called the number April had dialed, but never got a response. Had it all been a dream? Maybe April and her missing sister were just figments of her imagination?

But then, on Monday morning, shortly after opening time, as Carmen set out a display of fresh rosemary rolls—and Joseph was fielding the breakfast crowd over at the Amish diner—April was suddenly back, standing at the bakery counter, helping herself to samples, gobbling up little bits of bread as though she hadn't eaten anything in days.

"Hey there," Carmen said, trying to act casual. She slid a plate with a cranberry-walnut roll on it to April. "It's hot out of the oven. Want some butter?"

April nodded.

"Any luck with your sister?" Carmen said as she buttered the roll.

"Her name is Rose," April said. "And no."

"Have you considered calling the cops?"

"Not doing it," April said, with a mouth full of bread.

"Listen," Carmen whispered, leaning over the counter, "the cops are going to find out that there's a missing person. And if they find out you knew and didn't report it, they're going to suspect you."

Carmen had no idea what she was talking about. Everything she knew about police procedure came from TV and movies. But it didn't stop her from speaking confidently. She figured the kid needed a push.

"You listen to me. You're gonna have to deal with cops, one way or the other," Carmen found herself saying, mimicking the shows she watched. "The question is: you gonna be the worried sister or a suspect? Your choice."

April nodded slowly.

"I'll think about it."

"Good," Carmen said, switching back into her real voice. "Now . . . how are you doing?"

"Me?" April said, and made a sound that was either a laugh or a whimper—Carmen couldn't tell. "I'm a complete and total mess."

April told Carmen a story that made her head spin. April was doing a court-ordered Narcotics Anonymous program; if she missed any NA meetings without a good excuse, it was over for her. She would be immediately arrested and forced to serve six to twelve months in prison. The judge who'd ordered it had literally pointed at April and said, "Don't mess up this time, or you're going to find yourself in a tiny prison cell. I promise you that."

The words had chilled April to the bone. She'd had a lot of run-ins with the law, from drug possession charges to small-theft charges. So far, she'd managed to avoid jail time. But her luck was running out and she lived in deep fear of prison.

"I can't go there," she told Carmen. "I know what goes on in there. I got friends who've told me. And I'm claustrophobic. I can't be in a locked room. I can't do it. I'll go insane."

But, at this point, April was in the system. And being in the system meant there was a force as strong as gravity pulling her toward prison. She hadn't missed any meetings yet, or the community service that she had to do, but she'd been very close a few times. She'd passed the first urine test. But it had been a huge battle for her. She didn't think she'd be able to keep up for six months.

"And it's not just 'cause I'm messed up," April told Carmen. "I mean, okay, I am messed up, right? But it's more than just that."

Last week, for example, April had had a chance to get a job—making sandwiches at a Subway—but the manager had wanted her to start on a night when she had to do community service work and he wasn't willing to be flexible. So she lost that chance. And another prospective employer, in another shop, almost physically kicked her out when she said that she'd have to work around her NA meetings and community service work. A temp agency laughed in her face when she arrived underdressed and without a resume. April was broke and becoming desperate.

"I don't know what I'm doing wrong," April said.

Everything, Carmen thought to herself. You are doing everything wrong.

And then, of course, there were her problems with men. April had a type: beautiful boys, who were incompetent criminals. And who were just generally incompetent. "This kid didn't even know how to tie his shoes," April told Carmen of her last boyfriend.

Carmen snorted.

"I'm serious, though," April said. "He literally didn't know how to do it right. I taught him Bunny Ears. Like I'm his momma. He got mad at me when I did it but then he totally used it."

He also didn't know how to put on his sweatshirt. He

would struggle inside of it, like a chick trying to hatch from an egg. April used to watch the process with amusement. It had endeared him to her. She was charmed to see this tough guy vulnerable for a moment. But, later in their relationship, when things had gotten bad, she was far less amused.

He'd developed a pill addiction that ravaged his body, his mind, his life, and, eventually, April's life, too. Her first major court case came from her involvement with him: she was caught helping him break into a house—the house of his best friend's mother, no less— to steal some jewelry and electronics to sell to support the habit. April had figured that, if she helped him, he was less likely to get caught. Instead, she was the one who got caught.

Carmen listened quietly to everything April was telling her. Suddenly, without thinking, she said, "How would you like a job here at the bakery?"

Even as the words were coming out of her mouth, she found herself thinking: What am I saying? Someone tells me 'I'm an addict and a felon' and my response is 'Hey, come work for me'? Carmen was beginning to doubt her sanity.

But she'd made the offer, and April's response, she had to admit, was rather winning. April ran around the counter and threw her arms around Carmen's neck.

"You don't know how much this means," she said, as she hugged Carmen. "I'm gonna work really hard. Not gonna let you down."

Carmen really wanted to believe it.

* * *

April was late to work the next morning. And, the next day, she arrived even later. After a week, it was official: April was incapable of arriving on time. Each morning, she had an excuse. Of course, Joseph, watching from afar, didn't mind. He was just thrilled that April was suddenly working only a hundred feet away from him. It seemed like a gift.

Carmen didn't mind April's constant lateness either— she was just worried about what it meant: what other problems April might bring to the bakery.

The ongoing situation with Rose's disappearance made Carmen very nervous. What kind of mess was that? At the end of the workweek, April had finally called the cops to report the disappearance. Carmen had made it a condition of her working at the bakery—but she still didn't know the exact reason April had been so uptight about the police to begin with. Was April concerned about her own legal problems or was there something more? Carmen wanted to know the answer, but she also really, really did not want to know. She didn't want to hear something that would pull her deeper into whatever kind of mess this was.

Carmen watched, nervously, as April made the rounds in Reading Terminal Market, chatting with the market's shopkeepers about her missing sister, asking them to help keep a lookout, and giving them an official "Missing" poster. Carmen wanted to help with the search, too. But every time she saw April, wearing a Metropolitan Bakery apron—which April had done intentionally so she would be taken more seriously for these little meetings—Carmen winced. All around the market, April's troubles, whatever they were, were becoming synonymous with the bakery and, by extension, with Carmen herself. Carmen knew these shopkeepers well, and she knew that they would want no part of whatever kind of trouble was behind Rose's disappearance. She knew that they, like Carmen herself, worried that this mess would eventually intrude on their businesses.

One afternoon—the day before the police had come to take April's statement—Carmen noticed April standing by the door, watching something outside the bakery.

"Come here," April said, motioning to Carmen. "Check this out."

Carmen and April watched a young, tall Amish man posting Rose's "Missing" posters on a wall across the way, next to the Amish diner. They watched as he posted another one on the door to the market itself. And on a pillar in the middle of the market. And, then, on another door. The Amish man, in fact, had an entire stack of "Missing" signs under his arm, and he was posting as many as he could, on any surface he could find.

Carmen sighed.

"April . . ."

"I had nothing to do with this!" April said. "I didn't even talk to the Amish diner people about Rose. I have no idea where he got the signs."

Carmen gave April a skeptical look.

"I'm serious," said April. "I didn't say a word to them. I'm kind of afraid of them."

Carmen and April watched for a few more moments as the man continued to cover the market with pictures of Rose.

"I mean, I didn't say anything to them before," April said, breaking the silence. "But I guess now . . . I will? I mean, that guy's weirdly cute, don't you think?"

Carmen rolled her eyes and drifted over to the bakery counter. "Back to work, kiddo," she shouted from behind a pile of bread loaves.